THE FORGOTTEN AND THE FANTASTICAL 2

Also by Teika Bellamy

<u>Editor:</u>

Musings on Mothering (Mother's Milk Books 2012)

Letting Go by Angela Topping (Mother's Milk Books 2013)

Look At All The Women by Cathy Bryant (Mother's Milk Books 2014)

The Mother's Milk Books Writing Prize Anthology 2013: PARENTING (Mother's Milk Books 2014)

The Forgotten and the Fantastical (Mother's Milk Books 2015)

Hearth by Sarah James & Angela Topping (Mother's Milk Books 2015)

Oy Yew by Ana Salote (Mother's Milk Books 2015)

The Mother's Milk Books Writing Prize Anthology 2014: THE STORY OF US (Mother's Milk Books 2015)

Echolocation by Becky Cherriman (Mother's Milk Books 2016)

THE FORGOTTEN AND THE FANTASTICAL 2

Modern fables and ancient tales

EDITED BY TEIKA BELLAMY

Mother's Milk Books

First published in Great Britain in 2016 by Mother's Milk Books

Front cover image 'The Onyx Queen' copyright © Marija Smits 2016
Cover design copyright © Teika Bellamy 2016
Introduction copyright © Teika Bellamy 2016
Illustrations copyright © Emma Howitt 2016

Copyright of the stories resides with individual authors.

ISBN 978-0-9573858-9-4

Typeset in Georgia and Lt Oksana by Teika Bellamy.
Lt Oksana font designed by Lauren Thompson.
Printed and bound in Great Britain by The Russell Press, Nottingham,
on FSC paper and board sourced from sustainable forests.
www.russellpress.com

First published in 2016 by Mother's Milk Books
www.mothersmilkbooks.com

SPECIAL THANKS TO:

My wonderful family who beared with me as I sneaked away
at all times of the day and night to produce this book.
Emma Howitt for being one of the most imaginative, speedy
and talented illustrators I've ever worked with.
Angela Topping for granting me permission to use her poem,
'The Forest of Miracles' (from *The Fiddle*, Stride 1999).
All the wonderful writers who trusted me with their
"babies" — their precious stories.

CONTENTS

INTRODUCTION

The Forgotten and the Fantastical struck a chord with many of you, so much so that submissions increased fourfold for this, the next in the series, which made the choosing of the stories very difficult. Just the other day we completely sold out of the first book. I am quietly confident that *The Forgotten and the Fantastical 2* will be met with enthusiasm as, clearly, there is an appetite for fairy tales that feature strong, but real, women.

This book's alternate title could have been 'Mirrors' because when I was reading the submissions I noticed that some of the writers chose similar themes or even the same traditional folk or fairy tale as source material. But still, each story is very different. And it is this originality that delights me so much. Mothers, stepmothers, or absent mothers often feature in the stories, and breastfeeding is there in the background, sometimes the foreground. Mirrors and trees become characters in their own right, and wild spaces — jungles, forests and the sea — are magical places that call to both writer and reader. The heroines and heroes of the tales are flawed, yet determined, and as with the best fiction we see something of ourselves in them, even if the situation the protagonist finds themselves in may not reflect our own reality.

So once again, I invite you to breathe deep and to enter the world of the forgotten and the fantastical...

Teika Bellamy, Spring 2016

Rumpelstiltskin

by

Rebecca Ann Smith

Rumpelstiltskin

Once upon a time, in a faraway land, a miller and his little daughter lived alone in a millhouse on the edge of a village. The miller loved his little girl, but in the house where he'd been born, love was a rare and exotic commodity, like silk or spices from the East, and faced with the heat of his love the miller found he did not speak its language or understand its customs. So he made sure the little girl was fed and clean; he taught her to work hard, and for the rest he ignored her and let her run wild in the fields and woods around their home.

But sometimes, late at night in the alehouse, and after a glass or two, the miller's love was made liquid by ale, and there it found a voice.

'My daughter,' he would slur to the baker, or the cooper, or the landlord, 'she's bright for her age I tell you. A tiny scholar. She knows all her letters, even at the tender age of four.' And the baker or the cooper or the landlord would smile to himself, and let the miller talk, for he knew it was hard to be both mother and father to a little girl, and that the language of love came clumsily to a man with big hands hardened by work.

So the miller worked during the day and drank in the alehouse at night, and when he could find her he gruffly gave his daughter work to do. And when he could not find her, for she was off in the woods or the fields, then he would sit on his poor hard chair by the fire and dream about what she would become. And their lives were simple and poor, and perhaps a little lonely, but they lived them.

One evening in the alehouse, the miller was boasting to the cooper and the landlord when a stranger, an odd little man, entered the cosy, dark room and found himself a stool by the bar.

'And I'll tell you something,' the miller was saying, 'it won't be long before she can do all reckoning for the mill. I asked her, just this morning, if a hundred weight of flour costs nine pennies, and the baker takes a third of a hundred weight a month, how much is his bill for a year?' He stopped to take another swig of ale.

'And she knew it?' asked the cooper.

'Aye, she did.'

'She'll be an asset to you, that one,' said the landlord.

At the end of the bar the stranger laughed.

'Reckoning, is it?' he asked. 'How old is this child?'

'Ten this month,' said the miller proudly.

'And what else can she do?' asked the little man, motioning to the landlord for another round of ale.

'Why, thank you, sir,' said the miller. 'My little girl, ah, what can she do?' He sighed with contentment and settled into his favourite topic of conversation. As he talked, he felt his chest puff up and he held his head up high. And every humiliation he had ever suffered, and every beating he had ever taken was nothing to him now, as he was a man with pride in his heart.

After several ales and a lot of encouraging 'ah's and 'oh's from the landlord and the cooper, the stranger said, 'But it seems to me that spelling and reckoning are of small use to a girl, and knowing the names of the birds in the sky, or singing a pretty song, or making a clever remark, why, those won't put food on your table. All your talk is of fancy diversions, and there was me thinking you had a child of unusual talents secreted away in the mill.'

'But she does have unusual talents,' said the miller, feeling the wound even through the effects of the ale.

'What then?' asked the little man.

'She's a girl of such skill with a spinning wheel,' said the miller.

'Spinning?' snorted the little man. 'Every idiot girl in the kingdom can spin.'

'Not like my daughter,' said the miller angrily, 'she's a girl of such skill she can,' he paused for a second to think, unsteady on his high stool, 'why, she can even spin straw into gold!'

The cooper and the landlord laughed and shook their heads.

'You lie,' said the strange little man.

'It's the truth,' said the miller, insulted.

'How much will you wager?' asked the little man.

'What?'

'A wager, for a demonstration. Indeed, I would pay good money to see a girl who could spin straw into gold. How much do you wager?'

'I will not take your money, sir,' slurred the miller, in drunkenness and fury, 'my wager is my honour.'

'So be it,' said the little man, getting up to leave. At the door he turned back, producing from his coat a small parcel of straw, which he left on the floor between them. 'I'll return tomorrow night for the gold.'

Angrily, the miller swallowed the remains of his ale and made for the door. The landlord and the cooper exchanged looks as they watched him leave, thinking that by morning all would be forgotten.

'Daughter,' called the miller the next day, and she came to him, her dress dirty with mud and grass stains, a bunch of wild flowers in her hand. Her father was unusually fierce this morning, glowering at her, and holding one hand to his head as if in pain. She stood before him, very still, small and wary.

'Daughter,' the miller said again, 'today you are free from your tasks in the house.'

The miller's daughter could have leapt with joy, but she

knew from her father's harsh tone that this was not a reward for good behaviour.

'Yes, father,' she said meekly.

'Instead,' said the miller, 'you are to take this to the spinning room,' he handed her the small parcel, 'and you are to spin it into gold.'

'Yes, father,' said the girl, puzzled. She wondered what the rough paper contained, and how she would spin its contents into gold. She took the parcel and went up to the spinning room.

Several hours later, and bitter with frustration, the miller's daughter admitted defeat: spinning straw into gold was beyond the powers of even her imagination.

Which was when she noticed the little man, sitting on the three-legged stool by the spinning wheel, grinning at her expectantly.

'Do you need some help?' asked the little man.

'I do,' the miller's daughter admitted, 'but I don't think you'll be able to help me. My father wants me to spin this rough straw into gold, but I haven't the first idea of how it might be done.' She looked at the broken straw strewn on the floor and added miserably, 'In fact I'm not sure it can be done.'

'Anything *can* be done,' said the little man, 'it's just a question of knowing how. And some things can't be done in the common way. That's how you've got yourself into a muddle.'

'Can you show me how to do it?' asked the miller's daughter.

'No, no,' said the little man, 'that I won't do, because it's my secret, and no amount of watching me would teach you. But I'll do it for you if you like.'

'Oh, yes, please,' said the miller's daughter, 'that would be very kind of you. You see my father seems to want this very much, and I don't know how to give it to him.'

'I'll need payment,' said the man, 'something of yours, something valuable.'

The miller's daughter looked downhearted. 'But I don't have anything,' she said, tears starting in her eyes.

'Your shawl,' said the little man, leaning over to look at it more closely, 'I'll take that.'

The miller's daughter stopped crying and looked at the little man. When she realized he was serious she had to stifle a laugh, for her shawl wasn't valuable at all. She wasn't even allowed to wear it when visitors came to the millhouse, because it embarrassed her father. It was old and tatty, and she had patched and mended it with odds and ends of fabric she found about the house; one patch cut into the rough shape of a ladybird and sewn on with fat black stitching, another in the shape of a robin. Around the bottom she had embroidered the flowers of the hedgerow, but it was poor thread and rough work, and only in her imagination did the weeds stand out as fine flowers, dog rose, campion and honeysuckle. Still, she loved it, and it had taken hours of work, studying the forms she saw around her in nature, copying them and adapting her designs for embroidery.

The little man must have sensed her hesitation. 'It's your choice,' he said.

The miller's daughter looked at him. 'I don't have a choice.'

'You always have a choice.'

'But my father,' said the miller's daughter, and started to cry all over again.

'I know, I know,' said the little man, kindly, 'don't be ashamed to tell me, you see I've heard it all a thousand times before. He's cruel to you, and if you don't do what he wants, the consequences will be terrible. He'll beat you, or starve you, or sell you to the gypsies.'

'Oh no!' said the miller's daughter, shocked. 'He never

beats me, or starves me. And the gypsies are quiet, gentle people who live in beautiful painted wagons.'

'What then?' said the little man, growing impatient.

The miller's daughter thought carefully. She imagined her father's face if she went downstairs to tell him she had failed. He would be hurt, sulky, disappointed. He mightn't speak to her for days. His faith in her would surely be crushed, perhaps never to be recovered. She loved her tatty shawl, with its wild, colourful patches and lovely embroidered flowers, but she loved her father more, and she wanted his approval. She took off the shawl and gave it to the little man.

He put it on, picked up a handful of straw, and set to work. The miller's daughter watched him, amazed, as he fed straw into the spinning wheel. Wide-eyed, she saw bright gold collect around the bobbin, as the embroidered flowers of the shawl faded into nothing and the patches turned from lady-bird and robin into shapeless rough brown.

When the little man was finished he gave the miller's daughter the spool of gold and she rushed down to her father, barely stopping to thank the little man with the dull, brown shawl around his shoulders. Downstairs, her father was slumped unhappily in his chair. But as he saw his little girl come into the room, the bright gold reflecting its light onto her face, he cried tears of joy.

'My daughter,' he said, 'my little girl,' crying into her hair and kissing it. And the miller's daughter, who wasn't used to kisses, soon found that she was crying too.

And that would, perhaps, have been that. Except that news of a girl spinning straw into gold will spread quickly in a village, and soon the villagers were coming to the millhouse with straw and commissions, a wedding ring, an anniversary plate, an ornament for the mantelpiece. They paid the miller well for his daughter's talent, and the miller soon became a wealthy man. And while there was little need for gold in a village such as theirs, news spread to the neighbouring villages, and even to the towns, and people travelled from far away to bring straw to the miller and his little daughter. The strangers stayed in the alehouse, where the landlord built some new rooms to accommodate them, and where they ate his food and drank his ale while they waited for their gold to be ready.

The blacksmith started up a sideline fashioning gold, making bracelets and brooches, learning to craft fine chains and set stones. And it wasn't long before people were coming, not with straw or a commission, but simply to stay in the famous village and perhaps leave with a trinket or two. So the blacksmith was happy, and the landlord was happy. The cooper increased production of barrels and the baker increased production of bread and pies, so they were happy as well. And the miller was the happiest man in the village, for his wonderful, talented daughter had brought fame and fortune to them all, his honour was saved, and not only could he finally replace the roof of the millhouse, but he could repair the stable block too. He still worked at his mill, for a village needs a miller, but he took on a boy to help with the backbreaking work, and at night he dined with his daughter on roasted pheasant and fine wine, brought daily to the millhouse by the landlord's wife.

And the miller's daughter, was she happy? In truth she was happy enough. She settled into a pattern of spending her days in the woods and the fields, or swimming in the river, watching the plants and little woodland animals, or sometimes just lying on her back staring up at the sky. She spent much of her time in her head, making up stories and songs, and keeping a journal, which she kept hidden in the hollow of a tree. In the evening she would come home and wash, and then serve dinner to her father. They would eat together in the new dining room and afterwards she would go to the spinning room with the day's work of straw to be spun.

Every evening as she entered the spinning room, the little man was there, waiting for her. She paid him with everything she had made that day, and he always accepted her payment. A painting here, a collage of pressed flowers there, a sketch of a tree or a hedgehog. As he spun, the paint on the paper would fade, and the pressed flowers would crumble into dust. But the miller's daughter knew she would never be short of paint or paper or ink or thread, because now they were rich, and her father loved her.

As the years passed, she settled more and more into writing, and the little man seemed to appreciate her words. She would sit on the floor and read to him, and as he listened to her words and spun, the ink lifted off the page and vanished, and the paper disintegrated in her fingers. She wrote poems and stories, comedies and tragedies, ballads and histories, epic romances and domestic observations. She wrote plays about the characters in the village, and tales of imaginary creatures from other lands.

Yes, she was happy. Everybody loved her and was proud of her; there was a lot of status in being the only girl in the kingdom who could spin straw into gold. The village boys looked at her with admiration, and the village girls with envy. She was nervous of forming too close an attachment to any of them (for what if they learned of her terrible secret?) but she enjoyed their admiration all the same. And so what if she sometimes had nightmares about being unmasked for the fraud she was? And so what if she sometimes found the pressure unbearable and ground her teeth in the night? When she was up in the spinning room, reading her stories, she would see the look in the little man's eye and would know that she had his attention. She would read out a tragic scene, her voice shaking with emotion, and see a tear careering down his cheek. She heard him laugh out loud at a joke she made, or saw him sigh or smile, and she would think, *He likes it, he likes it.*' But nobody else saw these stories. They were just for the little man, and once they were read, and converted into precious gold, they vanished.

One day, when the miller's daughter was eighteen years old, a well-dressed man on a thoroughbred horse rode into the village, clutching a small bundle of straw. Very soon the news was being whispered at every hearth that he was a messenger from the king, sent to find out about the miller's daughter, and to test her powers with a new parcel of straw.

That night the miller's daughter's imagination was fired by the news of the strange visitor to the village.

'No reading tonight,' she told the little man, full of passion and confidence, and she proceeded to tell an epic tale, in rhyming couplets of iambic pentameter, of a poor miller's daughter with amazing talents, who was wooed and wed by a king.

The little man was mesmerized, and as he finished his spinning he said, 'Did you make that today and learn it?'

'No,' said the miller's daughter, proud and excited, 'I just made it up on the spot. It was like I held out a hand in my mind for the words, and they came to me, and I spun them into verse.'

'Could I hear it again?' asked the little man, but they both knew the words were lost.

A month later an invitation arrived from the palace. So the miller and his daughter travelled several leagues in their new wagon, to be the guests of the king. They exchanged nervous glances as a servant showed them to their luxurious quarters, and cried with delight to see the fine clothes that had been laid out for them to wear at the banquet. That night, as they dined on rich food and wine, the miller's daughter listened to her father's proud boasts while the king set out his commission. As she looked from her father's face to the strong, handsome face of the king, she knew what she had to do.

Back at the millhouse she unpacked the heavy bundles of straw and waited for the little man.

'This is a lot,' he said, 'a night's work. Do you have enough to pay me?'

The miller's daughter opened a satchel, and took out a sheaf of poems.

'That won't last the night,' said the little man.

Smiling, the miller's daughter took the rest of her work from the satchel, a few sketches, several stories, and some little wooden carvings.

'Still not enough,' said the little man.

The miller's daughter smiled to herself again, for she had foreseen this moment. From the satchel she produced her diaries, taken from the secret hiding place in the tree. She saw the little man's eyes gleam with desire.

'You don't have to do this,' he said, 'it's still your choice.'

But the miller's daughter knew she had made her choice, and she didn't hesitate. It was a lot of work, but she could always make more, and besides, there were far more important issues at stake.

By the end of the night the miller's daughter's voice ached from reading, and the spinning room was awash with gold.

So as everyone knows, the miller and his daughter became famed throughout the kingdom and the king asked the miller for his daughter's hand in marriage. The mill was left in the care of the hired boy, and the villagers came out of their houses to wave goodbye to the famous pair as they set out once more for the palace. The wedding was the finest the kingdom had ever seen, the talk of every town and village for months to come. The miller settled into a grand apartment at the palace and his daughter, the queen, set about learning her new duties. She had banquets to organize, the huge household staff to command, a husband to please and care for. She was so elated, and so busy, that she barely noticed the months passing, or the changing of the seasons, or the fact that she rarely had time to walk by herself in the palace grounds.

Then twelve months after the wedding, the king came to his new wife and took her hand.

'My darling,' he said, 'I have a favour to ask you.'

'What is it?' asked the queen, all smiles.

'There are problems in the south. The neighbouring kingdom is encroaching on our territories and I fear that there is going to be a war. I need money to protect the borders of our lands, and to put down the rebellious barbarians. Spin straw into gold for me once more, fill our coffers, and help in the fight for our kingdom.'

The queen was uneasy at the thought of war, and instinctively she clutched the small round of her belly. While her husband had been busy with his advisers, he hadn't noticed her sickness in the mornings, the dreamy way she sometimes looked into rooms around the palace, imagining them for a nursery. If her husband was away at war, who would be there to comfort and protect her when the baby was born? But she knew what she had to do, and that evening took herself off to the spinning room of the palace.

The little man was already there, amongst the many bundles of straw. It was a year since she had seen him, and she couldn't fail to notice his hungry look.

'Dear friend,' she said, welcoming him graciously, although she was nervous, 'we have a job to do for the good of the kingdom. We are going to war, and the king needs money to equip and pay the soldiers.'

'I care nothing for the kingdom,' said the little man, 'borders and disputes mean little to me. But I will spin this straw into gold, if you can pay me.'

'Of course I can pay you,' said the queen haughtily, to cover her fear. 'I know your taste, and this palace is full of fine work. I can offer you a carpet, woven in the East with the most intricate designs, or a sculpture cast in bronze or carved from marble.'

'I don't want those things,' said the little man, 'you know what I want.'

'Or books,' the queen continued, 'a whole library of the greatest works of our kingdom's greatest writers, poets and playwrights. I will sit here all night and read to you.'

'No,' the little man hissed, 'you know the rules.'

And although they had never been stated, the queen knew that she did.

'I've got nothing,' she said quietly, 'you have no idea how busy I've been, between running the palace, and caring for my husband. I'm a queen now, I have responsibilities.'

But the little man wasn't interested in her responsibilities.

'Make something here and now,' he said, 'like you did before.'

'I'll try,' the queen said, and reached out in her mind for the words. But out of practice as she was, and unnourished by the fields and the woods and the river, no words would come.

'Then I'll take that,' said the little man, glancing at her belly, while the baby inside ducked and swam like a fish.

The queen turned pale, and sat down on a jewel-inlaid chair. 'You can't,' she said.

'As ever, it's your choice,' said the little man, 'but you have nothing else to give me.'

The queen considered her options. She would tell the king she couldn't spin the gold, and he would forgive her. But all of a sudden she saw that without the gold, he would not. Maybe, she could run away, go back to her village, to work and bring up the child. But she would be nothing, nobody, she would have no money, and her father would be shattered by her shame. And without the gold to protect the kingdom, they would be invaded by the southern barbarians, all their lives would be different forever and many would be lost.

But this way, she would save herself, and her father, their rich lives and their position; she would keep her secret and do her duty to her husband. She would save the kingdom.

'Yes,' she told the little man, 'take it.'

'It's not enough,' said the little man, 'I need your ideas,' he paused to savour the words in his mouth, 'your imagination.'

So the queen sat through the night on the jewel-inlaid chair, telling stories of her future life with the child, singing lullabies to it, imagining its tragedies and triumphs, its face, its voice, its warmth in her arms, its fears and how she would have calmed them, the adventures they would have had together.

And in the morning the palace spinning room was full of gold and the baby was gone.

For seven long years the war raged. Everything was diverted to the war effort: horses were taken from farms to carry the cavalry, metal was fashioned into swords and arrowheads, food was sent to the troops. Many babies cried for hunger during those years and many mothers lost their sons.

The king seldom returned from the front, and when he did he saw that the queen was not the bright young woman he had married. Her kisses held no comfort for him and there was no warmth in her embrace. So he took himself away to his war rooms with his advisers to plan his next campaign. There were no banquets to organize since the war had started, and one by one the male servants were taken away to fight. The queen tried to keep herself busy managing the skeleton staff, and she spent the rest of her time avoiding her husband and her father.

Then one day, news came to the palace that the war had been won, the barbarians defeated. The queen set about organizing a huge victory banquet and the news spread that people from all over the kingdom were invited to join in the celebrations. A makeshift village of marquees was erected in the palace grounds, jugglers, storytellers, poets and musicians were invited to provide the entertainment, and an army of cooks was employed to make and serve the food. The night of the banquet the queen dressed in her most elegant gown. She took her father's arm as she walked out through the palace gates to await the arrival of her husband. A cheer went up from the crowd as his horse was sighted, and as the king rode up to the palace gates, the queen threw out her arms to greet him.

The feasting and entertainment went on late into the night, and at last the queen turned to her husband, smiling and said, 'My darling, the war is over, and it is time for you to rest. Let us retire now to my apartments.'

But the king turned away from her. 'How can you, a woman, know the sacrifices of war?' he said to her bitterly. 'All you know is feasting and gold. You are a stranger to me now.'

The queen looked around at the drunken crowds, dancing and singing, welcoming their men folk home. But even in the midst of the revelry she could sense the pain of loss, her people's and her own. She returned to her apartments alone, and found the old, tattered garments she had worn when she arrived in the palace eight years before. She took off her gown, and pulled on a faded yellow dress and leather boots, and wrapped a worn, woollen shawl around her shoulders. She packed some food and some coins into her old satchel, went down to the stables, and led out one of the king's horses. And in the chaos of feasting and dancing, nobody noticed her leave.

For many days and many nights the queen rode through the war-ravaged kingdom, stopping at this village and that, sometimes spending a night in an inn, sometimes sleeping in a hay barn. Sometimes she took a little money from her satchel to pay for food, although most days she was too weary and heartsick to eat. She travelled over hills and through valleys, on roads that snaked along beside bright rivers and green fields surrounded by hedges, but the world had no beauty for her now and the colours were dull to her eyes. When she came to her home village the people there watched her curiously, a wild-looking woman on a wild-looking horse, but they did not recognize her as the miller's daughter that they had once known, the little girl who could spin straw into gold, or the woman who had become queen.

So she rode on, heading south, into unknown country, asking in the villages where she stopped if anyone had seen a strange little man, travelling like her. Often the villagers were wary, or knew nothing. But sometimes a man, a woman or a child would report having seen him, and the queen raced on, chasing her quarry. So the days turned into weeks and the weeks turned into months, and the queen never let herself think of the husband and father she had left in the palace. As she crossed the border into the land of the barbarians she saw that their lands were as war torn as those of her own kingdom, and she found the people the same as the ones she had left behind.

One evening she found herself in a small village, much like her own, and decided to stop at the alehouse for the night. Looking into her satchel, she realized she had no money left to pay for food for herself or for oats for her horse.

'Do you have any work for me?' she asked the landlord. 'I can cook and clean, make beds and build fires, chop wood if you need me to, but I have no money and I need food for myself and my horse so I can continue my journey.'

The landlord was a kind man and when he looked at the queen's torn yellow dress and into her thin, but still young face, and saw the lines of care and pain written there, he wondered if she had lost a husband or perhaps a child, in the recent war.

'We're in need of a pot-boy,' he said, 'or a pot-girl perhaps. Can you do that?'

'Yes,' said the queen, and set to work.

So the queen turned pot-girl stayed at the alehouse for several days, working for her keep. And as the days turned into weeks and the weeks turned into months, she realized that she didn't want to leave the little village, or the poor alehouse, or the kind landlord, and she worked on. She worked from morning until night, scrubbing floors and tables, cleaning down the bar and washing the pint pots, serving bread and cheese to travellers. And at night, when the last of the customers went home and she was weary from the work, the landlord would pour her a glass of ale and they would sit by the fire and talk.

She listened while the landlord told her stories of the war, his lost brothers and cousins, of the hardships they had suffered and the battles they had seen. And the pot-girl curled up in a big armchair by the fire and listened. But she would never tell her own stories, no matter how the landlord coaxed her. On Sundays she would accompany him to the church, and after the service would go out alone into the fields and woodlands on the other side of the river, letting herself smell the sweetness of the honeysuckle, or watch the new leaves form on the trees in spring, sometimes swimming in the river under the boughs of the willow. And sometimes, with the sun low in the sky and her wet hair hanging down her back, she would sit on the banks of the river and weep.

One day a strange little man came into the alehouse and settled himself at the bar. The pot-girl hung back in the kitchen, watching. His face was unchanged, and although ten years had passed since their last meeting, she recognized the hunger in his look. When the little man left the alehouse at the end of the night, the pot-girl wrapped her shawl around her head and shoulders, and snuck away to follow him.

It was dark, the night lit only by stars and the newest of crescent moons. The pot-girl followed the little man out of the village, over the bridge across the river, through the fields and into the woods. She followed him until she reached his makeshift camp, a rough lean-to in a little copse, where he settled down to build a fire. When the fire was blazing, the little man threw back the hood of his cloak and danced around the flames, laughing and shrieking.

The pot-girl stepped out of the shadows and into the firelight to confront him.

'You stole from me,' she said.

The little man stopped dancing and looked at her, trying to place her face.

'I did not,' he said finally. 'We made a bargain, but the choice was always yours.'

'You tricked me,' said the pot-girl, 'you took away my words and my youth and in the end you took away my child.'

'No,' said the little man, 'I never tricked you. I simply gave you what you wanted.'

'It isn't what I wanted,' cried the pot-girl, 'at least, it isn't anymore.'

'There's no going back,' said the little man, 'I don't have the things you paid me with for your precious gold. I used them up and now they're gone. If you want those things again you have to remake them.'

'I can't,' said the pot-girl, 'I've forgotten how.'

'Then you need to remember.'

'How?' said the pot-girl.

'I don't know,' said the little man, 'it isn't my talent. All I can do is make gold. If I could make stories and poems, if I could make paintings and songs, if I could make babies, I wouldn't need people like you.'

The pot-girl slumped down by the fire, defeated. She had believed that someday she would find the little man, and on that day her losses would be restored to her. In the glow of the firelight she wept, grieving for everything she had valued so lightly and given away with so little thought. In the morning she went back to the alehouse to speak to the landlord.

'Where have you been?' he said. 'I've been worried about you.'

'I have to leave,' said the pot-girl, 'I have a long journey to make, a husband and father to find, and wrongs to put right.'

The landlord sighed. 'If you must go, then you must go. But before you leave, tell me why.'

The pot-girl filled her lungs with a deep breath, took the landlord by the hand, and led him to the armchairs by the fire. And in the pale yellow light of the morning she told him her story, the words reaching out to her from the air around them, finding their place in her head and in her heart and on her tongue. And when she was finished, she bid the landlord goodbye, saddled her horse and rode out into the world again.

Hansel's Trouble

by

Lindsey Watkins

Hansel's Trouble

Twice my brother has lived in a cage. Now, he is incarcerated at Her Majesty's pleasure in a brick-built labyrinth of corridors and cells. There will be no more trouble from him. No more drugs, no more drink. No more larceny, burglary or robbery. No more anti-social behaviour. No more rows or fists or stolen fivers. While he is inside. And then, when he has done his time and his haphazard rehabilitation, he will come out and he will start again. Drugs, drink, larceny, burglary and robbery. Anti-social behaviour. Rows and fists and stolen fivers.

How did I escape? I do not know. Some trick of genetics, perhaps? I will not chance it for the next generation. I keep my baby close. She spends her days in the sling and the nights in my bed. Always against me, all she knows is my skin — its smell and feel and taste. When the wind howls through the wild pines and the owl hoots its mourning call in the wickedness of the night forest, I hold my baby close and, unaware of anything but love and warmth, she sleeps. And, God willing, this is what we will do for now. Until she has taken what she needs from me in milk and security, I pray that I'll be spared.

Unlike my own mother. She met a wolf one day on her way home through the forest. My brother and I were still scampering on all fours like the beasts themselves when the hairy devil crossed her path and gobbled her up. We went out to look for what was left but there was nothing — not even the velvet ribbon from her hair. Nothing but a wolfish snarl carried on the wind.

So each morning after that, Father would bring us a basin of milk from the old nanny goat. Draw the bolt, he would say, when he went out to work the land. My brother and I would sup our milk and cling to each other at the hearth, hopeful that the magical dancing flames would return to smother last night's ash before the winter numb in our toes spread to our hearts. But there is no cold like a mother-hole, that gaping void.

Into the trees, into the wood, I stride, with my bundle of baby tied to my chest. We stop in the clearing where sunlight warms the bluebell bed and I settle on a pine-stump nursing chair. My baby feeds and I munch on the cheeses and fruit from my basket. But as I sit and nurse and eat, a shadow falls. The bluebells sound a toll of miserable memory: a childhood picnic. One, and then another...

One: the first picnic. Through the wood we had scampered, my brother and I. Father and Stepmother following. (The wife-hole had been filled now... and the mother-hole? No. Nothing can fill a mother-hole.)

Naïve to the absurdity of a bleak November picnic of stale scraps, I had skipped and sung my way along the narrow woody paths. Mother-abandoned, I hadn't expected to be father-abandoned too.

Even then though, my brother had known. Always sensitive to a look, a mood, a secret, he had filled his pockets with pebbles and made a stony trail for us to follow home again.

Left under a tree to hear the sound of chopping wood abate and then cease, we had made a bed in the dead-leaf sludge of forest floor and, soaked in the sodden sorrow of our own tears, we had slept.

In the black and silver of a full-moon night, we had been woken by the rattle of our own shivering bones. Along the pebbled trail we had trotted, tumbling through the cottage door in a sleepy heap of skin and bones at some pitchy, witchy hour; the rasping snores of our abandoners had been our welcome.

So then we come to the other one: the second picnic. A final family outing on an icy February day. A feast of two stale crusts served on a bed of snowdrops, a damp rug of grubby earth.

A father's remorse is inconsequential after an abandonment. The child clings all the tighter, but the seed of horror has been planted. And when a child has been abandoned twice, once by mother, once by father, a third time is only to be expected — if the mite has anyone left to undertake a third.

So on that icy February day we both understood what would happen. With no pocketful of pebbles, it was morsels of his precious mouldy bread my brother threw. And I watched as a hungry chaffinch bobbed behind us, gobbling up each grey morsel. Again we were left under a tree to picnic on scraps and lick the salt from our tear-stained cheeks. Again we rested and woke to the sounds of nighttime and aloneness. Again, we tried to scamper back to the cottage, to search for some forgotten nugget of love, hidden under a mattress or at the back of a cupboard.

But the crumbs had gone.

We hurried panicky and panting back and forth past half-remembered branches, faintly familiar tree stumps and clumps of winter foliage. And then, as the dim light of a dreary dawn turned the blotted canopy above a dull green, hopelessly, wearily, we wandered. And we wandered for a week or so before the glint of a frosted sugar window shimmered between the trees.

And thus, the first incarceration. For all her cunning, the witch of the conjured cake abode had a struggle getting my brother in the cage. Brought up on bread and boiled cabbage,

35

we were not accustomed to the effects of sugar: my brother climbed the four walls, reaching for candied cornices with a burst of vigour hitherto unknown, while she hobbled below wielding her catching net of twisted twine. But the sugar made him sick in the end of course — all down the fireplace, as he scaled the chimney. And then, all of a sudden, the energy wore off and he crumpled in the grate.

So while I scrubbed and polished and fetched and carried and dusted and chopped and stirred, my brother crouched in his cage. The novelties of feasting and fattening made up somewhat for the inconvenience and discomfort of sitting folded in a barred box. And each morning as the witch came to check the progress of her porky prize, he would press his fatty rolls to the back of the cage and proffer the spindly chicken bone to be squeezed and assessed.

How long would the patience last? My patient serving, his patient munching and squatting. Her patient appetite, waiting to cook and savour the succulent flesh of childhood. This was how long: three months, three weeks and three days.

And then a day when she could wait no longer. A day when my own skinny frame was looking like the nearest she might get to a tender cut of meat. Waking at dawn, all toasty for once, I knew for sure that something was awry. When I went down I discovered the source of the heat: a fire burning hot as hell in that devilish kitchen grate. And the witch standing all snakily sly at the hearth. *Test it*, she said. *Get in girl and test if the oven's hot.*

Well there were demons dancing in the heat of those prancing flames and I wasn't about to join them.

In there? I can't get in there, I can't climb, I can't fit. In there? How so?

How so? What too slow for this even, get in the oven, stupid child, like this!

Like this, like that and so it was that she showed me how, and as she did, I showed her how to shut the door on her bony behind — bang!

So sugar-high and pockets bulging with witchy wealth, we left that cake house and trotted back along the twisting wooded paths. No pebbles or crumbs to guide us but there it was: our father's cottage. And delighted he was to see us (the children he'd abandoned twice). Overjoyed. And with stepmother dead as a dodo and our stash of stolen riches stuffed into our pockets, it should all have been happily ever after.

But delight and joy and wealth were not enough. Not enough for poor Hansel, my brother. The seed of horror, planted once upon a time, had grown into a twisted, choking vine that strangled any attempt to trust. And so, sometime after the first incarceration, sometime before the second, came the drugs, the drink. The larceny, burglary and robbery. The anti-social behaviour. The rows and fists and stolen fivers.

And while I carry my baby and calm and feed and soothe and rock, I hear in the rustle of the wind-rattled leaves, the cry of a boy, a baby, calling out for a wolf-savaged mother, calling out for a father who twice left his babies alone to starve. And thus, thrice abandoned: there is no happily ever after.

Grimm Reality

by

Ana Salote

Grimm Reality

I was thirty years old when I saw the fairy. It wasn't in some secret glen. It wasn't at the bottom of the garden. I didn't enter another world through my wardrobe. I saw her when I pulled the curtains at dusk.

I live in a ninth floor flat at the Elephant and Castle. It was the coldest winter day for a decade and my boiler was broken. I had never seen my windows iced over before. Although I was cold to the bone I thought how pretty they were. Like a child I made pictures from the ice patterns. There was a long sharp nose and jagged ears; it could have been Jack Frost. And there was a tiny figure — I took a breath; it looked like a fairy, incredibly tiny and frozen to the window pane. How beautiful, how detailed and how impossibly real. As I looked more closely a wave of something like shock or panic passed through me. This wasn't an interpretation, a Rorschach blot or Christ in a split aubergine, it was something real.

I was afraid to lose sight of this thing which seemed to me infinitely rare and precious and frightening but I needed to bring it in. I couldn't reach through the upper window so I backed away, fetched a stool and spatula, and checked again. I expected the illusion to have disappeared, but no, there was the tiny grey face in apparent foetal slumber, the perfect arms and legs. I opened the window. A biting wind blew into my eyes and hair. London rumbled below. I hung out of a tower block window and carefully scraped a fairy out of the ice with a spatula.

I lay her on a wad of tissues and watched as the ice crystals melted. She looked limp and weak and fragile. One leg was twisted at a strange angle like a spider lifted from bath water. I tried to lay her out more naturally but she was too delicate for my fingers. I fetched some tweezers and clamped them round her leg, but again I found them too clumsy. Perhaps if I warmed her she would revive. I folded more tissues around her and fetched my hair dryer. No, that would be like placing her in the path of a gale. Instead I wrapped myself in blankets, set the tissues on my lap, shielded her with my hands and watched. Like a mother with her newborn I could not marvel enough. Still, at some point I fell asleep.

I opened my eyes on the cold, dim room. It is never fully dark in London and the hall light was on. I sat forward, ready to sleepwalk to the bedroom. What a strange and lucid dream I'd had. I looked down at my lap with a wry smile of remembrance. She was still there, her figure just showing against the white of the tissues. She had moved to a kneeling position.

'Oh my God,' I breathed. 'You're real. Don't try to move. I'll get the light.' I put her on the table and angled the lamp above her. Her little face came into focus. 'Look at you,' I said, incredulous. I touched a forefinger to her back. 'Oh look, are these your wings all folded up?'

She looked over her shoulder and partly spread her wings, pleased at my delight. Then she spoke. 'What a story,' is what I thought she said. Her voice was very small.

I saw that she shivered. 'I'm sorry about the cold; I can't afford to have the boiler fixed.' I gabbled platitudes.

'I see. You are poor, like a goatherd or a widow with many children?'

'Yes,' I laughed, 'but it's my own fault.'

'Did you gamble with your mother's cow?'

'Not exactly. I'm a shopaholic.'

'I don't know that word.'

'It means I can't stop shopping.'

'Like the girl in the red shoes who can't stop dancing?'

'Something like that.'

'So you need to break the spell. What is the enchanted object?'

I showed her my credit card. It lay on the table next to a pair of scissors. 'I wanted to cut it up but I couldn't.'

'It doesn't look magical. Who cast the spell? Do you know?'

'I hadn't thought — marketers I suppose. They make you believe they have the secret of happiness.'

'You must go to another market, even if you have to travel further.'

'That's not so easy. They all use the same tricks.'

'You had better take me with you and see if I can help.'

'I will in the morning if you think you'd like it but I want to know about you. What's your name? What are you? How did you come to be stuck to my window?'

'I'm Lunette.'

'Funny, I'm Lynette.'

'You must have read stories as a child, Lynette: of fairies, elves and leprechauns — the little people?'

'Some,' I skirted.

'Well I'm one of them.'

And although I asked her many more questions she kept referring back to stories and what I ought to know if I had read them and thought about them properly.

'I'll be honest,' I said. 'I skipped straight from hungry caterpillars to Vogue. I mean tutus and glitter just didn't do it for me.'

She examined her own dress which was twinkly with a pointed hem.

'Don't get me wrong. You carry it off all right. I'll tell you who I did rate — Cruella de Vil. She had a sharp look and a sense of her own style.'

'And what if a few puppies lost out?' she said sadly.

I had never given much thought to the puppies.

It was near midnight when she urged me to go to bed saying she didn't want me to shape-change, her day had been exciting enough. I had to agree with that. I made her comfortable on the bedside table inside a quilted evening bag. Like children at their first sleepover we couldn't rest, closing our eyes and opening them again to whisper one more confidence. Eventually my eyes stayed shut.

I dreamed of all the children's tales I knew of but had mostly never read. Gruff ducklings waited under dank bridges for ugly goats, Hansel tracked Snow White to a cottage by following bear droppings, Rapunzel let down her hair from a tower block. In the morning I woke from pure excitement. My own fairy was still there and she was ready to shop.

We walked into the morning sun. The ice had melted. I told her she must stay in the phone pocket of my coat. I left the zip half open so that she could look out. I felt excited, mad, favoured, magical. When I glanced down at her face it was filled with the most avid curiosity though sometimes she stopped her ears against the traffic roar.

I took her to my favourite shop. I hadn't been near this shop for weeks, imposing my own no-go zone while I struggled to pay off some debts. The window display had changed and it was all so desirable. The new season's colours were perfect for me. My heels clacked on the wooden floor. I stroked a top, ogled a boot and sniffed a scarf. I could see Lunette's concerned face between the teeth of the zip.

'I think you'd better leave now,' she said. 'Let's go where we can talk.'

We stopped for a latte, sitting in a quiet corner.

'That's the first time I've ever left that shop without buying something,' I said.

'I saw nothing of value or beauty. I expected rich brocades, cloth of gold and glass slippers, not dull peasant clothes. Your eyes must be enchanted. Tell me what you think you see.'

'Well fashion is an art. It's all about self-expression. Did you see that slate dress? It was so edgy.'

'Yes, the edges were very rough. A fairy tailor would be ashamed of it. What else do you see?'

'I see — I see style and glamour, and a new, better me. And all I have to do is put this bit of plastic in a machine and punch a number.'

'And what about the puppies?'

'The puppies?'

'The children who labour for endless hours in windowless rooms to make the clothes for you. You were in a great hurry to leave your childhood. They don't have a choice. You must have read 'The Little Seamstress', surely?' I shook my head. 'Anyway,' she went on, 'I can help with the secret number. I know a counter spell. It will lock the number in your mind so you can't reach it. Do you want to try?'

I thought for a minute, then shook my head. 'No need,' I said. 'You already broke the spell.'

'Really?'

'Really.'

'With reason alone? I never believed in reason before.'

'And I never believed in magic.'

'This really is the best giant story. It beats nurseries, parks and rabbit holes. I hope he writes about you again.'

'Who?'

'Fairy Grimm. He's a famous writer of giant stories.'

'And he wrote about me?'

'Of course, or we wouldn't be here.'

I looked puzzled.

'Don't you understand? If I'm in your story, you must also be in mine.'

My world pitched even further sideways.

'A writer in your world and a writer in mine are writing the same story,' she said. 'That doesn't happen often. We're very lucky.'

I saw him then in my mind's eye: Fairy Grimm with night cap and candle, quill wagging, as he scratched my name on a page made of tree bark.

'This story that we're in,' I said, 'what's it called?'

'The Strange World of Elephants and Castles. Good title isn't it? That's what drew me. I haven't seen either yet but I expect they're around?'

'Where is the giant writer?' I asked the fairy.

'Nearby,' she said, 'nearby.'

Bear, Hare and Ptarmigan

by

Julie Pemberton

Bear, Hare and Ptarmigan

There was once a woman whose sister died. The woman knew her sister would die when she looked into her garden and saw a blue cedar tree swaying in the wind. Its branches shook out filmy white sheets of spores that billowed and spread to fall unseen across the garden. Then the woman saw how it would be so with what grew inside her sister's body. When her sister came to visit her, the woman embraced her but lightly, so that her sister would not feel the knowledge of death in her arms. Instead, she took her sister's blue velvet coat into another room and held it tightly and wept into its collar, *Do not die, do not die.*

But her sister died, even so.

The woman missed many things about her sister but it was her voice she most longed to hear. She remembered the sound of her voice and she kept a set of sentences her sister had once worn. Sometimes the woman took these sentences out from the place she kept them and polished them. Sometimes she put fragments of them in her mouth and rolled them over her tongue to catch the taste: sweet, sour, bitter. But what she really wanted was to know the taste of *now* in her sister's mouth. Then in her sad anger she would put the sentences away with a roughness that made them tangle and break so it was harder to piece them together when next she wanted to polish them.

One day the woman travelled many miles to a place of her childhood; limestone crags with caves where people had lived in the days long before long ago when the world was covered in ice.

There was a log cabin where travellers like her could rest before walking paths beside caves whose mouths had long since been barred, chained and closed to any passer-by. The woman drank some water in the log cabin then pushed open the wooden door to begin her walk along the cave paths. Instead she found herself in another room with rough-hewn planks along ceiling, wall and floor. Another wooden door stood at the end of this empty room and the woman opened it. It led to a tunnel with walls of crusted limestone and the woman had to stoop to pass through. It was dark but she could see flashes of light coming from an arch so low she had to crawl to reach the innermost chamber.

It was a gigantic cave with narrow stony paths that sloped steeply like curved spokes to a high platform. On the platform was a huge grey throne and on it sat a thin grey figure. His sharp eyes glittered in his gaunt face as he watched the woman approach and he wrapped himself more closely in his chain mail cloak, as he prepared to speak.

'You are looking for a voice.'

Sparks flew from his mouth and bounced fleetingly on the chain mail before disappearing into the darkness around him, 'A voice that speaks of now.' His voice grated and crackled with light again, 'Come closer, woman.'

The woman climbed a curving path to the platform and saw a pile of bones on the floor in front of the Greyman's throne.

'Sit with me,' sparked the Greyman. 'We will have fire.' As he spoke he caught the shower of sparks in his hands and threw them on a pile of wood beside the bones. The fire blazed and the woman saw pictures on the walls of the cave; running men, running horses, running deer. The Greyman picked a bone from the pile and handed it to the woman. An arc of broken light flew from his mouth, 'Bear, hare or ptarmigan?'

The woman felt the weight of the bone in her lap.

'Bear,' she said, and the Greyman took the bone from her and threw it in the fire.

A huge bear rose from the fire in front of them and roared.

'What does it say?' asked the Greyman. The woman saw milk leaking from the bear's nipples.

'She says, "I want my cubs, give me my cubs."'

The bear stepped out from the fire and kissed the woman with its soft-lipped muzzle then fell as a bone back into her lap.

The Greyman took another bone from the pile and gave it to the woman. In a shower of sparks he asked, 'Ptarmigan or hare?'

The woman felt the hollow lightness of the bone in her lap.

'Ptarmigan,' she said, and the Greyman took the bone from her and threw it in the fire.

A plump white bird flew screeching into the air above the fire.

'What does it say?' asked the Greyman.

The woman saw the bird pluck anxiously at its feathers.

'She says: "Oh white winter plumage! Yet I feel the heat of summer, I can be seen, oh I shall be seen!"'

The bird flew from the fire to the woman's shoulder and kissed her with its blunt beak then fell as a bone back into her lap. Then the Greyman took two bones from the pile and his words crackled with shards of light.

'Hare? Or sister?'

He gave one of the bones to the woman. She felt the lean strength of the bone in her lap.

'Hare,' she said and the Greyman took the bone from her and threw it in the fire. A hare leaped long and lissom in the flames.

'It does not speak,' said the Greyman, 'but what does it say?'

The woman saw the sad longing in the hare's eyes as it gazed yearningly into the darkness of the cave's ceiling and she felt tears on her face.

'"Where is the moon?" it says, "I want the moon."'

The hare leaped to her side and kissed her with its restless mouth then fell as a bone back into her lap.

Then the Greyman threw the last bone into the fire and the woman's sister rose up from the flames. Her hands were full of flowers and she threw one to the Greyman who caught it with a laugh that sent a whirl of sparks chasing round the cave.

He turned to the woman, 'Your sister does not speak, but what does she say?'

The woman looked into her sister's eyes and saw the meaning of every word her sister had ever given her.

'"Love," is what she says. "Love, love, love."'

Then her sister walked from the fire to sit between the Greyman and the woman, kissing her softly with her mouth warm from the fire.

Her sister took the woman's head gently in her lap and began to tell her stories. As she spoke, tiny silver drops of light fell from her mouth and into the woman's ear. She told the woman stories of the bear, the ptarmigan and the hare: legends of loss and grief, vulnerability and fear and the ceaseless disquiet of impossible longings. They were sad tales but her sister stroked the woman's hair as her voice dropped rhythmic as a lullaby into the woman's ear and she was soothed. The last of the fire died and all was darkness in the empty cave.

The woman woke with her head on the table in the log cabin, the bottle of water beside her. She pushed open the wooden door and saw the way she had come to get there. As she began the long journey home she seemed to hear her sister's voice lapping at her ear; she knew with luminous clarity what her sister would say about everything that had happened, the *now* of it. And this was true for all the times after, sad, glad or happy times, singing times or sighing; she knew what her sister would say. Her voice would fall silvery-soft and shining into her ear.

The Jungle Goddess

by

Anuradha Gupta

The Jungle Goddess

Down in the valley, the drums had begun to sound at the first sighting of the moon. Their rumblings, gentle at first, had grown louder and bolder with each beat so that they were now rising and falling; giant waves crashing, echoing against river and rock in a dizzying frenzy.

Up in the mountains, deep in the woods, Gungun covers her ears as the sounds explode around her, scattering the birds and the beasts into the night. She crouches low, sinking deeper into the shadows, away from the glare of the moon. She cries out, as the tremors begin to rock her body. The noise stirs up ghosts. Ghosts of another night like this; a night almost forgotten. Unbeckoned, the ghosts come to her, one by one. A wedding, a bride, a girl dressed in red and gold, a moon, beating drums, beating drums. *Go, go,* she hears the villagers saying. *Go on child, the Jungle waits for its bride.*

Go. Go now, they had urged her impatiently, then begged desperately. Oh, how they had begged, she remembers, willing her to take that first step towards her new home while she had stood, teetering on the edge of two worlds, swaying to the beat of the drums.

Her father had remained frozen at a distance saying nothing, his back to her, to them, while her mother had wailed; her grief inconsolable. Gungun had stood for an eternity on that edge, blinded by her tears and deafened by their cries. Then, because there was nowhere else to go but away from it all, she had run as fast as she could and as far as she could into the wilderness, into the arms of the Jungle that was waiting.

She listens to the drums now, she hears their beats climbing the mountain slopes, higher and higher, rising above the tree tops, above the jagged cliffs and above the mist, reaching for the silver moon as it floats up into the purple sky.

Gun-Gun, Gun-Gun, Gun-Gun, they seem to call. The sound of her name, like all else that was once hers, is only a memory and memories come and go like fireflies.

Gun-Gun, Gun-Gun, she hears the drums calling to her again, trying to coax her out of the forest. Gungun leans against the tree and steadies herself. She clutches the vine that is wrapped around the trunk and digs her nails in, refusing to let go. But they keep calling, insisting, until, like a woman charmed, she begins to follow them.

Down in the valley, the villagers have gathered to celebrate the coming of spring. A spring they all hope will be blessed by the Goddess.

It is the last full moon of the passing winter and as every year they light a bonfire, pour offerings of butter and milk into the flames, beat their drums, sing songs, pray for a good harvest and wait for the omens. The sweet calling of a cuckoo bird before dawn, the flowering of jasmine in the night, the spontaneous ringing of temple bells, a falling star, the howling of wolves and cawing of crows; the signs are many.

The village folk, like their ancestors before them, have learnt to read these signs — to look into the very hearts of their gods and goddesses. Hearts so deep, so mysterious that they hold within them all the secrets of all the worlds. Secrets that are revealed only to the very brave. And they are a brave people.

But tonight as they gather around the fire, they are, once again, afraid. An unending pain fills their hearts. The wrath of the heavens has held against them for too long.

It was right in the middle of the harvest season, the villagers recall silently, so many long years ago, that the dreadful curse had struck. Not one of them would ever forget how house upon house had been laid to waste as mother after mother lost a child and then another and another. Such fury had been unleashed upon them as they had never seen nor heard of. They had tried every medicine and prayer known to them, offered all they had in sacrifice and avowed penance but nothing, nothing would appease the gods.

When the priest and the healer had given up, the villagers had turned, defeated and in despair, to the village astrologer. What is wrong? They had wanted to know. Have the gods no mercy? Was nothing sacred anymore? Their tormented souls had cried.

The astrologer in turn had turned to the stars for the answers. He had etched with great care the planets and constellations on the baked ground of his front yard, creating intricate patterns in the red earth with his stick, while the villagers looked on. Then he had taken a few cowrie shells from his waist pouch and cupping them in the palms of his hands rattled them, breathing little chants into them before rolling them on the floor. With a bounce and a thud the shells had landed randomly on the stars in the chart, dislodging bits of the flaking mud.

The astrologer had stared for a long time at what had come to pass on the dusty sky at his feet. He was old, older than all of them. No one alive remembered his father or mother but they said he knew things that ordinary men could not even imagine. He understood, they said, the workings of the heavens, the churning of the celestial oceans.

The villagers waited for him to speak.

And when he did, his voice was old and faded. The Jungle burns, was all he said at first. They did not understand. It was not the season for forest fires and all was quiet on the slopes.

But as he looked past them to the mountains beyond, they feared what his eyes, so cloudy with age, had seen.

'Such rage.'

The astrologer shook his head and clicked his tongue, pointing to the shells, which meant nothing to the villagers so they looked at him instead, their despair deepening.

'Only a woman can calm such rage,' he continued, the last of the embers flickering in his grey eyes. 'Everyone knows that without a woman all homes go awry and a Jungle is no different.'

A bride, he had said, is what the Jungle needed. A bride.

The council had chosen a girl of thirteen. A child, almost a woman, blessed with a rare beauty. Her birth chart, the astrologer announced, had the markings of divine stars. She was born to save them, he said.

It was the grandest wedding the village had ever seen, as befitting the gods and the bride was sent off into the forest to the beating of drums, in all her finery, to set things right.

With the lifting of the bridal veil, the curse was lifted too and the deaths had stopped. But the emptiness had remained. The bad omens had continued. Year after year when the drums rang out on the last full moon night of winter, all they heard were wild cries and howls from deep within the darkness that surrounded them. Then the sounds too had stopped. Now they waited and hoped for the good omens. For, eleven years on, the women were still grieving and barren.

*

Up in the mountains, Gungun does not know which way the sounds are carrying her but she follows them anyway. With each step the drums get closer and louder till she can no longer tell if they are beating outside or inside her; till she can no longer tell if they are real or a memory. And in that daze of not

58

knowing and not being, she stumbles eyes half shut and panting for breath out of the dark blue forest into the pale white moonlight.

The drummers drop their sticks and a silence falls over the crowd. Men and women, all turn to stare at the vision before them. Gungun, with her dark untamed locks tumbling down over her bare shoulders and breasts, adorned in nothing but a silver anklet, stares back absently at the blazing fire and the grey shadows that stand all around it.

The silver snake coiled at her ankle dances in the firelight.

The villagers watch mesmerised, nobody moves, nobody breathes, until an old woman rushes forward and falls at Gungun's feet.

'It's the *Vandevi*, it's the *Vandevi*,' she cries hysterically. 'Praise the Goddess of the Jungle,' she sobs loudly, 'for she comes to bless us.'

The spell broken, the men quickly avert their eyes and the women gather around Gungun. They lead her by the hand and seat her on a makeshift throne of bamboo. They garland her with flowers and anoint her forehead with bright vermilion. Turn by turn, they come and fill her lap with offerings of fruits and flowers. The fire crackles and spits. Someone blows the conch and then someone strikes a drum. It's time to celebrate, they shout. More drums join in.

Gungun flinches at their touch and closes her eyes. *What is this world?* she wonders. She does not recognise it and yet it reminds her of another she once left behind. *Look at me, I am Gungun. Look at me,* she wants to say. But her words, like her clothes, have fallen away over the years and lie withered like wild flowers on the forest floor. Her tongue moves and twists in her mouth trying to curl around the alphabet but the letters, swollen and heavy, are difficult to hold. She is filled with other sounds: the rustling of the forest wind, the chirping of birds, the buzzing of bees, the crying of wolves, the singing of the rain and river. She is filled with the Jungle.

Stirred by the sight of the young Goddess in their midst, the women begin to dance to the rhythm of the drums. They clink their anklets and thrust their hips deliberately, lustily. The men, drunk on the fermented brew of the mahua fruit and the beauty before them, watch their women, sarees askew and cholis drenched with sweat, moving round and round the fire. The men and women steal glances at each other and watch the Goddess, golden in the amber light, her skin glistening, her face bright. It is a bewitched night, fragrant with the first flowers in bloom and bathed in moonlight.

Gungun opens her eyes and looks at the strange shadows that flit around the fire, twisting, turning, merging, whirling, whirling without beginning or end as if a moment in time has come unhinged. And then it falls to pieces to the beat of the drums — dust, ashes, smoke, fire. Something unknown, unnamed, uncoils deep inside her and courses through her veins. Perhaps darkness, perhaps lightness. Her body begins to heave and convulse and she lets out a howl, a loud piercing howl that tears through the night and rips open the sky. The stars fall and the earth shakes. The drums stop. Gungun leaps up from her throne, turns her back to the spectacle and vanishes into the dark.

*

Afterwards, no one speaks of the night the Goddess returned. It lies buried in hushed tones and furtive looks. It was a blessed night, the women whisper sometimes to each other when they are bathing in the pond or collecting firewood, their bellies swollen with their unborn children. It was the night the Goddess came bearing fruits, they say.

60

Mirror, Mirror

by

Laura Kayne

Mirror, Mirror

Alexandria was seven when the carnival first set up camp in the woodland at the edge of the city outside the walls of her father's castle. From the nursery window the young princess could see the bright lights and colourful tents, and hear the unusual shouts and cries of the fair-folk that were like a foreign tongue to her, and just as irresistible and exotic. Alexandria, knowing only the inside of the palace, was captivated by this strange new world. The fair was unlike anything the young princess had ever seen, an unfamiliar land compared to her world of nurses, maids and servants in the vast castle. Even at such a young age Alexandria was keen to know of life outside the stone walls. The exotic and enticing sounds, smells and colours — so near yet so far — called to her. All day long she pestered her father to allow her to visit the carnival, scared this strange new world would disappear before she could learn of its wonders. But the king had forbidden her to visit the fairground, and even temper tantrums and pleading could not change his mind on this occasion. Her father refused all pleas, telling his beloved daughter that she was too young and the fair too dangerous. Despite the fact that he called her the apple of his eye, on this occasion the king was stern and no amount of begging or tears would sway him from his decision.

And so it was, in the way of many small girls who do not wish to disappoint their parents, Alexandria went to the carnival without her father's permission or knowledge. The castle was large and old enough to be a city of its own, especially to a small girl, with adequate rooms, corridors and passages to create a playground that would take her a lifetime to become bored of. A quick and studious girl, the princess had long since discovered more than one of the various tunnels and passageways hidden in the castle, and so one night, borrowing her nurse's cloak for a disguise and taking some coins left on a nearby table, she crept out of the palace and into the woods. Alien sights and smells overwhelmed her senses and she smiled in delight. How much more interesting than the castle was this secret place? The smell of roasting meats, sweet biscuits and strong smelling brews drifted on the gentle breeze whilst the doorways to tents flapped open giving her a glimpse of what was concealed inside. Old women offered silk cloths and sparkling red and blue baubles. The city children, who Alexandria was not allowed to play with, were running around the tents and stalls, with the older ones daring each other to ride on the wooden swings, shaped like boats, that flew into the sky and back. After eating her fill of sweets and failing to win a toy, the girl's attention was captured by a small oriental man inviting people to enter the Chamber of Mirrors.

The chamber was actually a maze, its walls lined with mirrors of varying sizes and styles. Long, twisted corridors led visitors towards the centre of the chamber. Lanterns were placed on the ceilings, throwing a dim and eerie light through the corridors of the maze. With very little light within the maze the reflections from each glass became mysterious and lifelike, as visitors would find it more and more difficult to separate the mirror images from real people. The lack of light created an eerie, mysterious feel to the place and often made it difficult to know exactly what or who one was looking at. Although all of similar sizes, the mirrors were all very different in what they chose to show the viewer. The twists and turns of the 'Chamber' and the placing of the looking glasses only added to the mystical effect, making some participants unsure exactly what they were seeing and what was a real reflection. Young Alexandria continued through the chamber, fascinated. The first mirror showed her reflection as tall and thin, the next short and fat. Others gave the viewer a large head atop a tiny body, in some she obtained huge hands or feet or eyes. One in particular gave a reverse image and Alexandria stared at this twin in amazement. Her long black hair was blond and unruly, her pale skin was ruddy and tanned, and her usual bright blue eyes were a rich and deep brown. The eyes of this other Alexandria gazed back at her as if in her own funhouse of warped mirrors. Without really understanding why, Alexandria reached out a hand to touch her twin, convinced she would encounter warm skin and bone and was startled when her mirror image did the same and they both found cold glass under their fingertips. Her look-alike shared her expression of surprise as she lowered her hand and moved away from the looking glass.

She smiled at her twin and watched this other girl return her gesture, feeling that somewhere, on the other side of the glass that separated them, there was a girl exactly her opposite looking at her own mirrored twin. It made no sense and the rational part of the girl wanted to deny the magic and mysticism of the Chamber of Mirrors but, as she backed away and turned to run out of the maze, the other, pure-child, part of her realised that something inexplicable had happened to her that night.

Time passed, as all things must, and Alexandria grew up. She learnt more about royal life and obligations and found less time for fun and magic. Pampered and wealthy she may have been, but this did not protect her from the difficulties of growing up. She wanted freedom — as all teenagers do — but having the king as a father meant this was easier said than found. With her mother having died when Alexandria was very young, the king had left the princess in the care of her nurses and maids who, fearful of losing their positions, took their roles very seriously. They ensured no harm would come to

Alexandria, even from herself. On the eve of Alexandria's fourteenth birthday the king announced that he would be remarrying. It was a political arrangement, for it did not look good for the ruler of the country to appear at too many state banquets without an appropriate companion. The daughter of an earl from a neighbouring land, herself only eight years older than Alexandria, had been given in marriage by her own father to the king.

The soon-to-be queen willingly tried to become friends with her new stepdaughter, being so close in age she believed the two of them could easily be companions, and they were by far the youngest of the palace household, barring the younger chamber-maids with whom they were forbidden to socialise. But Alexandria was jealous of her would-be stepmother — her skin was clear and her hair shiny, whilst Alexandria was trapped with the blemishes of adolescence. However, Alexandria had no choice but to attend the wedding, set for a month later and grudgingly had to busy herself helping with preparations.

It was a week later that the carnival returned to the city. This time, with the chaos of the wedding preparations, dress fittings and flower arrangements to be decided, the Princess found it much easier to escape the castle and visit the fairground. Again she disguised herself and kept to the shadows, for being older and more prominent in court she was better known to the king's subjects. Being both more cautious and more hurried than on her previous visit Alexandria made straight for the Chamber of Mirrors. The vivid sights and smells of the fair immediately reminded her of seven years earlier and her sense of magic and mystery returned. Her double was still there, just the other side of the glass, just out of reach; but Alexandria was still drawn to her twin, and felt that the connection between them had inexplicably grown stronger in her absence. It was her, her own reflection, and yet it wasn't. The smile on her double's red lips was playful and knowing, suggesting secrets Alexandria didn't have access to. The princess wondered what kind of life her twin led, what her life might be like away from the confines and restrictions of the palace walls. She laughed at her silliness and her reflection became just an image. Leaving the Chamber of Mirrors Alexandria felt some sense of reality return to her and so she began to search the stalls and tents for a suitable gift for the new queen. She passed displays of engraved rings and amulets, richly coloured and skilfully beaded robes and slippers and elaborately feathered headwear. Unsure what her stepmother's tastes were, she decided against these, annoyed at the difficulty of trying to find a gift for someone who had everything. And then, at the last small stall, almost overshadowed by its larger and more popular companions, she saw many looking glasses. Alexandria's decision was made for her as one golden-edged oval-shaped mirror seemed to call to her to buy it.

Years later, after legend had chipped away at the once-known truth and fiction was found to be more exciting than reality, people said that it was the mirror that was the truly evil one. But how can an inanimate object be good or evil? There are more ways and reasons than you may imagine, especially with items so closely linked to their human owners, their masters. Or maybe the masters are the servants. No one seemed to know exactly where this looking glass came from (for Alexandria said only that she was offered it), and this only added to the mysteriousness. Some said the mirror was once a witch, who, after losing a fight with a younger and more powerful sorceress, was turned into a mirror, forced forever to watch the world around her and never again participate. Others suggested the mirror was just a mirror, but enchanted by the witch so that it could be her eyes for her when old and less sharp in wits and observation. It was oriental in design, with elaborate markings etched around its edge and its thin gold frame. It was unlike any mirror the queen had seen before, and quite the most magnificent of the wedding gifts. The king himself paid it no attention, confident in his own authority that he looked his best, so he left the servants to hang it in the queen's chambers, laughing at the fact that his wife was in thrall of her own image. The king loved to guess how long the queen would spend in front of her looking glass, her maids assisting her in creating a persona suitable for the role of the king's consort, which changed with various state functions and balls. It was his duty, of course, to ensure that his queen was educated in such ways, that she knew how to look and behave as one who accompanies the ruler of the land always should. Unknown to him, the king determined his new queen's identity as much as she herself did.

The queen knew that she was beautiful, but also knew she was not as young as she once was. The mirror both heightened and calmed her anxiety. The need to be told one is the fairest of all is not wicked, but only human, especially when living in the public eye as the queen was. The pressure to maintain a public image was incredible, and unlike anything the new queen had faced before. Although many of the people did love her, criticism from some was fierce and this pale reflection from harsh crowds who still remembered and were fond of the king's first wife, saddened her, and then angered her. As the awkwardness of youth left her stepdaughter, the queen saw herself in the girl and longed for those days of youth and unquestionable beauty. Things had been so easy then, without the temptation to resort to magic of any kind to keep her fragile status within the heart of the king and the land. The few years of youth that Alexandria had on her grew in significance.

And so, the mirror watched all. Everything was reflected through its gaze, sometimes truly and at other times warped and deformed, as if a crack in the glass had changed the whole shape of the image seen there. The distortion was in the queen's mind, of course, but the mirror, being enchanted, chose to show her what her unstable mind wanted to see, and seemingly acted to increase this instability. The mirror laughed silently to itself as it showed her becoming old, fat, grotesque; her hair turning grey and her eyes dull while lines on her face and hands became more pronounced daily. Finally, she pleaded with the mirror to return her beauty and youth, and the mirror altered the image and did so. The queen was content once more, trusting this illusion. For a while.

Alexandria, meanwhile, the mirror showed in all her growing beauty, only emphasising the differences between them. The queen knew she could not compete. Alexandria gathered compliment after compliment, and took these to heart, making full use of her newly discovered femininity and loveliness, as all young women do, for this too is only human. And when Alexandria fell in love with a young woodsman the mirror — witch or demon it may have been — looked on at the proceedings with glee. From beneath its cold, plain face, hidden depths bubbled to the surface as it pushed the queen to more and more heights of cruelty.

Unknown to the queen, Alexandria had long been meeting with the young woodsman, Hans. When the queen discovered them together, she banished Alexandria from the castle. While appearing distraught, the princess was secretly overjoyed, being now free to spend time with Hans. The woodsman, gentle and uneducated, had quickly fallen for Alexandria's pure beauty, while she, basking in his attentions and adoration, had soon persuaded him to show her how to hunt and kill. He taught her the ways of the forest, and how to prepare food and often she surpassed him in hunting and tracking skills. She taught him about literature and music and they shared the household chores peacefully. She was strangely suited to life in the woods, and would often spend hours stalking deer to bring back to the woodsman's small but comfortable cottage for him to cook for her.

The mirror reflected Alexandria's happy life and showed the insecure queen how restrictive her own was in comparison. She spent more and more time in front of her golden-edged idol, needing reassurance that she was still beautiful. The mirror showed her ways in which to improve her image, and then, how to remove the competition. Alexandria was living in the forest, it told her, independent and contented. She had no pretty gowns or trinkets, her hair looked like it hadn't been tidied in days, yet it shone with health.

Since childhood the queen had been told she would be married to a king or prince and as a girl that had been her only dream. Now, having acquired all she had ever wished for, she wondered what else there was in her life. She grew ever more miserable and bitter. The king, loving her dearly but not understanding women and knowing that the running of the country had to come before family, bought her exquisite riches, threw feasts in her honour and told the servants to grant her every wish. His presents pleased his wife briefly, until she was once again shown Alexandria happily living in the depths of the forest and she wondered how the girl could be so satisfied with so little. Her stepdaughter had no maid, no one to cook or clean, no one to do her hair which was gradually becoming wild, unruly and curly in the sun and harsh elements of outdoor life with no way to tame it. Other changes were happening to the princess as well. The sun had at first turned her pale skin, unused to the weather after so many years protection inside the palace, red and sore. Now though it was becoming a light brown. The queen wondered if anyone in the castle would even recognise her if she returned. She was certainly not missed.

Realising that even the king did not miss his wayward daughter, the queen's first plan was hatched. Why not ensure she would never return?

'Kill her', the mirror whispered, 'and you will never have to see her image again.'

The queen concocted a tale of a wild and dangerous girl living in the forest, frightening young children — a threat to both herself and others. It would be a benefit to the girl to put her out of her misery and quickly and painlessly kill her. There would be a reward for the huntsman who killed her and brought her heart to the queen as proof of the deed. Some of the huntsmen who heard about this were, at first, reluctant to kill a girl, but the spirit of competition soon overcame their reluctance and they joined in the hunt enthusiastically. One of these was Alexandria's own woodsman. When he told her of the competition, the princess soon realised that she was the "wild and dangerous girl" and that her stepmother's dislike had grown to murderous hatred. She instructed Hans to take the heart of a pig that she had killed earlier that day and present it to the queen as Alexandria's own heart. The woodsman willingly did so, and returned to Alexandria with many gold coins which she spent on knives and new arrows for her home-made bow.

And so, for a time they were all happy. The queen, believing her stepdaughter to be dead, grew more confident in her own self and beauty, which caused the king to rejoice as the royal feasts were vastly more entertaining when the queen was happy. And Hans enjoyed watching Alexandria, assured and strong, hunting with her new weapons. Even the mirror was silently content, feeling its power grow over the queen and biding its time until it "suggested" its next task. But soon the mirror grew tired of her happiness and showed the truth. The queen screamed in rage. It was time for a new plan, the mirror whispered enticingly.

The queen had a recipe, passed down from her mother, of how to create illness in that most wholesome of foods, the apple. She knew that Alexandria would be unable to resist the gift of an apple, especially in the winter season. The palace's food stores were plentiful but the queen was sure that Alexandria would be short of food living in the barren forest. She picked the most innocent, wholesome-looking apple she could find, irresistible to anyone, and carefully concealed the poison mixture inside its juicy, red flesh. Making up a basket she decided it was time to visit her stepdaughter.

It was cold and dark in the forest when the queen arrived at the small cottage Alexandria and Hans shared. 'Alex', as the princess had informed her she was now calling herself, had been shocked to see her.

'You tried to have me killed!' she screamed, before slamming the door in her stepmother's face.

'Yes, but I was unwell then. I've been seeing a healer, though. He says that I was married too young, and unused to royal life my mind became... perturbed. But I'm feeling in good health now. Here, I've brought you a hamper of food...'

Alex was sceptical, but her stepmother seemed genuine and so she finally let her come inside. It was true that they could do with some more food supplies. The winter was not an easy time.

The queen and Hans greeted each other and Alex was pleased when this went well. The wine that Hans had made himself helped and the game that Alex had caught and cooked was delicious. The queen was impressed by the small comforts of their home, with its roaring fire and homemade furniture. But not one mirror adorned the walls. She questioned how her stepdaughter managed without checking her appearance, but Alex replied that she simply had no need to style herself when there were no members of the court around to judge her looks and clothes. The concept was so foreign to the queen that she immediately changed the subject. The evening was so pleasant that by the time she had to leave, the queen, without the whispering encouragement of the mirror, had almost forgotten why she was there in the first place.

'Thank you for the basket of fruit,' Alex remarked, wondering if she could come back to the castle for a few days of luxury.

'Oh, you're welcome.' The queen hesitated. 'You know, maybe I should return with some fresher apples. I don't think these are as nice as they look...'

The princess sighed. How spiteful to come bearing gifts and then to want to take them back!

'No, I think they look lovely. We'll enjoy them tomorrow. Goodnight.'

She practically pushed the queen out of the door and began to clear the table. Surprised as she was by her stepmother's gift of friendship, Alex had quickly learnt not to refuse such offers, and food would be scarce in the upcoming weeks. She remembered how tasty the imported fruit and vegetables bought by the palace were. The largest reddest apple was practically crying out to be eaten, temptation itself, and Alex couldn't resist a taste. Taking it from the basket she went to eat it, when Hans noticed her and requested an apple too. She passed him the one she had, with a smile, thinking again how handsome he was. He was no prince but he was certainly charming enough for her.

'This apple is delicious,' he declared, wiping the juice from his lips. He washed it down with water and then Alex looked on in concern as he began to choke. She rushed to his aid but he was turning pale, his face contorting. He sank to the ground, gasping for breath. Helplessly, Alex watched as the life seemed to drain from his body.

In the castle, the mirror watched silently and laughed tunelessly. The queen, distraught at the knowledge of what she had done, screamed and cried at the mirror to show her things as they really were. But this time the mirror chose to show only truth — the poor woodsman slowly worsening whilst Alex's happiness slipped away with him. The queen felt helpless and tore at the mirror, trying to destroy the image. But the mirror was resistant to her scratches and knew that it had full power over the queen. She looked into its dark depths and no longer recognised herself. The bitter, old woman staring back was not her. It was as if she had been a puppet, controlled by the need to become her image, and in the process had lost herself. The image facing her was no longer someone she recognised or wanted to be. She thought of Alex, no longer Princess Alexandria, living free from mirrors and expectations of appearance and duty. She had looked wild, happy and so different from the stern, pale young girl she had first met at the palace. Her hair was blond and curly, her skin a rich brown from the sun. She had changed more than her name, her stepmother realised. Now she knew that they could be friends, how could she face the fact that she had tried to kill her? And even though she'd failed in that, she was sure she didn't want Alex's lover to die either. She watched Alex throw the rest of the basket of fruit away. The mirror hissed in annoyance, even though it had still succeeded in destroying Alex's life, even if not by killing her.

'Isn't that enough?' the queen screamed at it.

'How could you have enjoyed her happiness? She should be here at the palace, with you, on show for the people,' the mirror said, not for the first time.

'Why? Because my husband says so? He's too busy with his Council to even care!'

'Because I say so,' the mirror replied softly, determined not to let its victim escape its thrall. 'Did I not help you obtain beauty, and did you not see how the people loved you? Did that, did I, not make you happy?'

'No,' the queen cried, seeing the truth at last. She picked the mirror up and smashed it to the ground. It shattered into seven pieces, cutting the queen's hands in the process. Her maids, alarmed at the noise, found her staring at the blood on her hands in shock.

Alex, meanwhile, had discovered that Hans was not dead, but that she could not rouse him. So she went to the only place she could think of for help. The carnival.

She ran through the fair, obtaining welcoming looks and smiles, and feeling a long way from the small, pale child wrapped in a cloak.

An old woman claiming to be a witch was peddling potions and spells and Alex went to see if she could help. She sat huddled over her small stall, peering suspiciously up at her visitors.

'He's been poisoned, has he? By a witch?' she asked, with a cackle, as Alex explained the situation.

Alex stated that she didn't believe in magic and witches, but that Hans was ill and she needed a remedy. The old woman stared at her and sat up straight.

'Thank goodness for that,' she declared. 'Foolish people like to think they're buying charms and spells from a "real witch" so I give them what they want. It's all in the appearance, you see. And they believe that what you show them is real. But I'm really just a healer. Here, take this vial of herbs and give it to your woodsman. It will revive him.'

Back at the cottage Alex quickly administered the healer's

herbs to the unconscious Hans. An hour later he awakened, the colour back in his face and feeling much better.

'You saved me!' he said.

'Well, there weren't any fairy godmothers around to do it,' Alex said with a laugh.

Seal Woman

by

Rachel Rivett

Seal Woman

Tonight! It will be my first time!

We swam, my seal sisters and I through liquid night, to where the Below place and the Above place touch. How dazzling the dark as we climbed the Dancing Rock and slipped and wriggled and giggled from our seal skins and lay them down on salty weed.

And while the sea sang and sucked and hissed and kissed we stamped our feet on stone and span and laughed for the sweet wild joy of it. Breathless with night; giddy with the prickle of starshine on bare skin.

And so I didn't see him.

When one by one my sisters put on their skins and the ocean opened to them I was left, lost, alone. My sealskin gone.

He held it in his hand.

My skin, my pelt, my soul.

He held my soul in his hand.

'Wife.' He hid my soul behind his back, held out his empty hand, offering me... nothing. I looked at him.

'Seven years then.' His voice was hoarse, his eyes full of me. 'Seven years; then you can choose to stay or return.'

I couldn't speak. Seven years! How many tide turnings is that?

And so we lived. He loved me well enough. But how can you give your heart to someone who has stolen your soul?

And then, oh wonder! A child came: bright shout of light, sweet chuckler, dimpled restless wave. He was my joy as my flesh and blood and bone began to fade, pining for the sea. He held my hand as I grew unsteady; he was my eyes as the light died in mine. 'Sing mother,' he would beg me. And so I sang for him the curlew's curling cry or the whale's long song until my voice grew parched and brittle.

He stroked my hand. 'You are not well, mother.'

I nodded, unable now to blink even a drop of ocean from my eyes.

Instead I clutched my husband's empty hand. 'Please, seven years have passed. Seven years and all these tide turnings. Let me go or I will die.'

'No!' It was a cry like the buzzard's: high and keening. 'Choose me.'

The child watched quick-eyed. 'Mother, I will make you well!'

And he ran down to the ocean in a slip and slither of sliding stones to find a pretty shell, a twist of wood, some sea medicine.

And so it was he found what I had lost. A ragged bundle, fallen from a cleft within the cliff.

He clutched it to him, his eyes large with mystery, and for a heartbeat he shone; my soul and his. One.

My heart shook, my hands trembled. Waiting.

Slowly his arms uncurled. He held it out to me. His hands full of it: my skin, my pelt, my soul.

He held my soul in his hand.

I clutched him to me, tight as tight. It frightened him: the desperate weight of my love.

'Mother, no!'

I picked them up, my child and my shining, shining soul, and ran stumbling over slippery stones to the sea.

He clutched at me. 'Mother, no!'

Clumsy, I fumbled into my sealskin, sobbing with pain and sweet relief.

'Mother!'

I took his face in my hands, placed my mouth gently over his and breathed once, twice, three times. Then I took his hand and slipped into the sea.

And so I returned.

Oh! How the water welcomed me, its moonsung tides and saltsweet song, its pull and pulse and kiss.

Oh! How my seal family danced to see us, how they played with my sweet child and showed him his other kingdom. Child of two worlds. One day he would come.

Or not. Let him choose.

And so we parted.

At the shore's edge, the crossing place where earth and water meet, I left him, watched him; swam until he was no more than a distant star, shining.

And now, sometimes, he comes to sit on Dancing Rock. Sometimes he calls me. And always I come, crossing sky wide seas to be with him.

My seal child. My soul child. My love.

Icarus

by

NJ Ramsden

Icarus

"Who is that man who travels round our mountain
Before death has given him the power to fly?"
Dante, *Purgatorio XIV* (trans. Sisson)

Once there was a man who wanted to fly. He'd tried jumping, but the fall onto barbed wire was unpleasant. He'd tried lowering himself down a ladder made of bed-linen, but the lights had picked him out. He'd tried burrowing like a fox beneath the outer fence but the dogs had caught his scent. Once, he'd tried to pass himself off as a German officer, uniform made of grey blankets and a stolen hat. The Kommandant, celebrating a haul of illicit brew, had shared it among his staff, but the guards on patrol had stayed disappointingly sober. So as not to spoil the party, the Kommandant invited him to sit with them in the mess. They drank each other's health in steins. He returned the hat.

*

Once there was a man who wanted to fly. It had not always been this way. The air had terrified him at first, even before he had risen into it. Heights, he maintained, were not a problem so long as you were safely at the bottom of them. The joke went well in the ranks. Death, like Love, was ever the comedian. During exercises, he had vomited his way to altitude and back down again, wondering as he parachuted across the plains what had happened to it. His pals thought him mad when he skived off later to scour the fields for evidence. He appeared at dusk, muddy and disappointed, but would not say why. He was afraid of admitting a fear of depth, of facing the unscalable. Even the best of their planes had limits. He was amazed the

85

bombers climbed at all, gargantuan as they seemed on the tarmac, spread out like sleeping dragons. He envied the men who piloted the smaller units, the fighters with exotic names and crinkled photographs of ladies in stockings tucked between inscrutable dials. He envied their solitude; he envied their dependence on accepted certainties — that the ladies would still be there when they got back, that the air would not give way beneath them, that the fuel would never run out — but he envied, most of all, what he would not permit himself: the acceptance of inevitabilities. They would die, those ladies too; the War would end, one way or another, some day or another. They'd been told Christmas, and not for the first time. But his inescapable end, along with unscalable emptiness, he could not allow, while being reminded daily of both.

*

Once there was a man who wanted to fly. He woke one morning earlier than expected and could not shake the feeling something was about to happen. He did not much like it. Through the window he could see rain, and the dim sea-grey dawn beginning its ascent. He busied himself counting raindrops and wondered how they fell. Later he would learn they were spherical; he had always assumed them shaped like tears. It seemed gravity favoured simplicity over pathos. He was not the only restless one; some of the other men had felt the damp in their bones and stirred before the bell. When it came, they had been alert enough for long enough to become tired by the end of breakfast. They took their places for briefing easily, with neither hesitation nor consternation. They took note of their mission. They chatted quietly in the open. They waited.

The cloud was low and thick, and the day lingered on outside their rising fuselage. He sat between Milton and Poe, the names he'd given two comrades before having spoken to either. Up front was Virgil, running over expected events like an accountant explaining taxes. Things were simple, but that didn't make them easier. Eventually Virgil stopped, unbuckled, and made a move. The plane began to empty. Only when he saw Milton's back dropping away into the cumulus did he realise it was his turn. *Muss es sein?* he thought, recalling Beethoven against his will; *Ja, es muss sein.* He stepped forward, and flew.

That is how he would have preferred to remember it — a harrier's swept arc, a graceful ballet of bird and cloud — but he plummeted ungainlily, flailing while he fell. His arms wheeled, his legs kicked, and the vicious winds shrieked away the vanishing throb of propellers. Invisible through this pale soup, the forest, he knew, was rapidly nearing. Some time passed; he unleashed his canopy; the jolt surprised his body more than his mind; he drifted, and a troublingly short time later landed inelegantly in the branches of a welcoming fir.

Some time passed.

*

Once there was a man who wanted to fly. He had been delivered into a world of surfaces, a cruelty he felt more severely toward the end of his life than the start. The meaningful world was planar, and one climbed or sank as providence allowed; one was on top of things, or beneath a thing, or stood by it; one could traverse the entirety of the globe and yet, like the darkest trenches of the ocean, the skies remained a mystery that mere observation could not conquer. There were scientists who postulated what lay outside the orbits of Man's experience while astronomers strove to map it; there were engineers, whose dreamed machines had begun to prick small holes in its boundaries; and there were those who, like him, threw themselves through it arbitrarily. He understood what orders were. Unable to release himself from the caul of his tree-caught parachute, he writhed, and waited, and writhed again. No-one came. He must have slept; he awoke to a prodding, and voices, and felt himself carried, though he could not have said more about it.

Later, he woke in a dark room, fastened somehow to a narrow trolley. His arms were free; his head was heavy; the darkness was soothing. This he would remember. A voice spoke softly, and he did not understand it. There was light, briefly.

Then, there was only the darkness.

*

Once there was a man who wanted to fly. Nature had prevented him from possessing the appropriate physiology, but had gifted his race with the capacity to overcome it. The process would take time. Healed of his wounds, he walked the corridors and stared from barred windows, paced the yard in the shadow of the clock-tower, and played games with the guards, who were mostly young and sometimes morally pliable. One of the Senior Officers had corrupted a sentry into bringing him razors. The officer wore a full moustache that curled at the tip like raised wings and had no intention of denuding himself. The razors became small saws, which turned bedboards into sewing machines. *The prisoners are taking a healthy interest in theatre,* remarked the Kommandant in his diary. *We have allowed them make-up and a small amount of material for costume.* The German play went well. Later that week a buxom but inappropriately hirsute fräulein was arrested forty miles away having sprung from a packing crate at the wrong moment.

Capture meant a month in solitary. He noted this. Someone threw a bottle at a guard one evening and he made sure to be fingered for it. It gave him time away from the others. The cells were on the other side of the castle to the prisoners' quarters, near the Kommandantur. If he stood on the rough stool he could see across the Tiergarten, over the river, and beyond the town. The walls were high, and the castle perched on an outcrop. He watched the birds turning circles above the flood plains, rising and falling in the grey air, rising and falling.

*

Once there was a man who wanted to fly. Escape had proved more difficult for some than for others. Some had been shot. Most had been returned. A few had made it. He had tried a half-dozen times, and never got beyond the perimeter. They received postcards from the lucky ones: *Dear Kommandant, enjoying the Swiss air. Yours, etc.*

He discussed plans with three other men. Not for the first time, they thought him mad, but only the truly mad would have maintained the poise of sanity, he said, and they believed him. They collected tools, made drawings, and built a partition wall from the ubiquitous bedboards and sheets, stretched and sized with contraband glue, and plastered over with the spoil from various tunnels. The attic was inspected almost daily but the Germans never noticed its upper storey was now some yards shorter. They worked at night, during exercise periods, through the bitter winter. They wore out their tools, replaced them, wore them out again. They repeatedly had to ask for more bedboards, but the Kommandant's curiosity never once overcame propriety regarding what they did to break so many. They would stand in for each other during parades, ducking between the rows of men already counted and swapping coats; they would take it in turns to hole up in the roof for a few days at a time, feeding on scraps bagged up by the others. One foul night the plan was almost rumbled by a French airman who had clambered up on the eaves and stopped to check his disguise in the attic's narrow window, only to find himself staring straight into another pair of eyes — the shock of it lost him his footing, and the sudden beam of a German searchlight traced the plumb-line of his descent.

*

Once there was a man who wanted to fly. News of the end of the war had arrived on the feathers of the wind, had been spotted in the way the rain fell, in the furrows on the brow of the Kommandant, in the vanishing of the remnants of the civilian population down on the plain. From up in the attic, he could scry through a cobbled-together telescope the scurrying away of what had been allowed to survive of normality, while each day the horizon grew darker. Energies were subdued, and in the clarity of an open-skied night, distant sounds of death could be heard rising like flakes of ash on the smoke. Everyone knew what was coming; nobody spoke of it — the Germans for fear of naming their end, the prisoners for fear of cursing the last of their luck. Business carried on as usual, almost.

He spent more time alone in the attic, working by cautious candle-light and the glow of the flames that were steadily approaching. Soon, he knew, the midnight sky would be brighter than these emaciated stubs, and their stink overwhelmed by ammonia, mud, grease — and the tang of American cigarettes.

His companions did what they could to relieve him of the burden of solitude but he was adamant and would not sleep while there was work to be done. He tried to impress upon them the urgency of completion, pointing at the sky, making gestures with his arms — but they were no longer convinced it was necessary. Rescue was on its way, they said. They should wait. Even the Germans just wanted it to be over, and were calmly, methodically preparing for departure, though they were uncertain in what state they would be departing.

Early one morning before dawn he decided he had finished and slept till the bombs woke him. A dark shape passed low over the roofline, growling at the windows, rattling weak plaster into puffs of dust. He stood slowly, procedurally; stretched, picked up a breaker's hammer they'd somehow smuggled out of the labour yard, and swung it at the props that held the gable-end.

Preparatory sketches, crude but careful, had paid off. The old wood gave way under the impact, the strain of all its years splintered into relief; the weakened roof sighed, its beams hacked back to a brittle skeleton that could no longer stand; and the whole end of the roof was gone, in a cloud of black shrapnel that from down by the river would have been indistinguishable from the shelling. He let the breeze blow through for a second, hawked the worst of the grit from his lungs, and stepped up to the ledge.

*

Once there was a man who wanted to fly. It had not always been this way, but the War had scarred him, confined him, and thrown him against his will into blind and fearful velocities. Beneath him, across the Tiergarten, over the river, spread across the burning plain, sprawled an array of machines ravenous for death and salvation, bronze and dark in the dawn's fire. The Americans were coming. It was time. He slipped into the gap in the framework of his labours, inhaled, and ran.

From below, it would have been difficult to describe exactly what one had seen. From below, it would have been difficult to see at all, through an air spattered with black and streaked with ochrous grey; but from between the bursting shells, through the unyielding battery, something pale and cruciform drifted slowly from a wound in the castle's flank. Some of the soldiers saw it and stopped; others glimpsed it as it slid between the dark stains their approach had spread upon the sky; others heard the shouts but could not make them out. Some said later it had appeared in a ray of spontaneous light that pierced the thunder they had made with silence; others said it was illusory and could be explained by psychology. Official documents recorded that a small white glider had been seen coasting high over the town, riding the currents of the cleaner air, above the smog of war, above the hot and sputtering embers of destruction — a small, white glider made of some fabric that glowed in the bright new sun, the RAF's concentric emblem painted upon it like a yell, and headed upwards, upwards, until it had all but vanished — a dot in the heavens, obscured by birds.

Lilasette

by

Ronne Randall

Lilasette

In a land far away, at a time long ago, there lived a queen with eyes as dark and cold as onyx and a heart colder and darker than her eyes.

She had a son, Marcus, a sturdy boy who romped and roamed the countryside and forest, chasing rabbits and scaring squirrels. His ruddy cheeks and rough ways made his mother smile with delight, and she hugged him to her bosom every night and morning.

As the boy grew, he became more restless and less patient with his mother's kisses and embraces. He turned to his father, who taught him to hunt with bows and arrows and fight with swords. As she watched the men ride out together, the old and the young, the queen knew that she would never again possess her boy as she had when he was small.

One year, when her husband's hunting dogs whelped, the queen took two of the puppies and made them her own. She spat in their food so they would take in her scent and be loyal to her, and she trained them to growl and show their teeth at anyone who came too close without her permission. Everywhere the queen went, the dogs went too.

But her two faithful dogs were not enough.

'I must have a daughter,' she said to herself. 'A daughter who will want to be like me, who will love and admire me, who will cling to me always.'

But the queen's loins were old and withered, and her womb had closed. She could no longer conceive a child, male or female.

As time went by, the queen's fierce desire to have a daughter ate away at her cold, dark heart. Then one day her most devoted servant told her that a young kitchen maid had a swelling belly.

'Bring her to me,' ordered the queen.

Trembling, with her eyes downcast, the kitchen maid stood before the queen.

'What is your name, girl?' the queen asked.

'Rose, your Majesty,' the girl answered.

'And is that a child growing beneath your breasts, Rose?'

The girl tried to shrink into herself, to protect the precious new life fluttering beneath her heart. 'Yes, your Majesty.'

'Who is the father of your child, Rose?' asked the queen.

Rose did not want to reveal this to the queen, for fear of what might happen to them both. So she said, 'The birds of the air brought the child to me, your Majesty.'

'Insolent wench! Are you so stupid that you don't know how you got your own baby?' said the queen. 'I will ask you again: who is the father of your child?'

This time Rose replied, 'The dark water of the lake brought my child to me, your Majesty.'

The queen was so angry now that she rose up and grabbed the kitchen maid by the collar of her tunic. Her snarling, slavering dogs lunged forward and stood at either side of the girl, their sharp teeth gleaming.

Twisting the rough wool of the tunic around her fist till Rose could not breathe, the queen hissed, 'I will ask you once more, you snivelling brat. Who is the father of your child?'

As she felt her heart pound and her lungs struggle, Rose feared for the life of her baby, so this time she gave the true answer: 'It is your son Marcus, your Majesty.'

'Lying whore!' the queen roared. She slapped Rose so hard that the girl fell backwards and crashed into a mirror, which shattered into a hundred pieces. Shards scratched at Rose's arms, legs and neck, and blood spattered onto the plush carpet. The dogs, wild with excitement, rushed forward, but the queen grabbed their collars.

'I should let them tear you to pieces for your filthy lies,' she snarled. 'But instead I will tell you this: you will be watched every moment of every day, until your bastard child is born. If it is a boy, he will be killed. But if it is a girl, she shall be mine — and you will be killed. Do you understand?'

Still sitting among the broken glass, Rose nodded mutely. A trembling servant helped her up and led her back to the kitchen.

Throughout the dark, cold winter, Rose's belly and breasts blossomed and grew. As she felt the child within her dance into life, her heart grew heavier and heavier, knowing what was going to happen.

One night in May, when the air was rich with the scent of lilacs, Rose knew it was time for her child to be born. As her womb pulsed and contracted, Rose kept silent. Struggling through her pain, she sneaked out of her quarters near the kitchen and went out into the palace gardens.

And there, beneath the lilac tree that stood below the queen's window, her baby was born — a beautiful girl with a soft pink mouth and wide, searching eyes. As soon as the baby uttered her first cry, Rose put her to her breast and nursed her, holding her close and safe. And as the little girl suckled, she took in the scent of lilacs along with the sweetness of her mother's milk.

'You are my Lilasette,' whispered Rose, 'and I will love you always.'

All at once the sound of barking ripped through the quiet night air, and the queen's dogs appeared, straining at their leads. A servant held them back as the queen herself, in a whirl of blood-red robes, hurled herself at Rose. With a swift, strong arm, she wrenched the still-suckling baby from Rose's breast.

The baby screamed. Rose screamed. The dogs howled and pulled and foamed at the mouth.

The queen handed the baby to a waiting servant, then drew a dagger from her sleeve. Swooping down, she plunged the dagger deep into Rose's womanhood and ripped out her womb. She threw it to her dogs, who devoured it greedily. Rose's blood sank deep into the earth, down to the roots of the lilac tree.

Leaving Rose to die, the queen turned and led her macabre procession back to the palace.

But Rose did not die. At dawn, as he made his way to the stables to saddle his horse for the day's hunting, Marcus heard a soft whimper from the garden. When he went to look, he saw Rose lying crumpled beneath the lilac tree.

He gathered her into his strong arms, and held her gently but firmly as he took her into the forest. There, deep in the woods, lived an old wise woman who made poultices of herbs to heal Rose's wounds, and fed her on tea and broth to make her strong again.

Marcus had not known about their child, for Rose had been too frightened to tell him. When he found out, and heard what his mother the queen had done, he vowed to take Lilasette from her and bring her to Rose.

'I will look after you both,' he promised.

But he never got the chance. As he made his way back through the forest, he was attacked by a wild boar and gored to death. Even the wise woman's strongest potions and poultices could not save him.

The queen went wild with grief when her son's torn and ravaged body was brought back to the palace. She was more determined than ever not to let her new "daughter", whom she had named Mia, out of her sight.

Mia slept beside the queen in her bed, the old woman's rattling snores her lullaby. She was not allowed out of the queen's chamber, even for meals, except on special occasions, when the queen showed off the little girl to visiting dignitaries. The queen put a heavy lock on her chamber door, and kept the key close to her bosom. She put bars on the window that looked out over the garden.

Mia was gentle and quiet, and learned to play contentedly within the confines of her little world. Often she was alone, her only company the few toys and books the queen allowed her to have. Sometimes the queen spent a morning or an afternoon with her, dressing her up in smaller versions of her own clothes and allowing her to wear some of her many jewels.

'We are a beautiful pair, are we not, Mia?' asked the queen.

And Mia always obediently replied, 'Yes, Mother, but your beauty far exceeds my own.' The queen had taught her to say this as soon as she had learned to speak.

'And do you love me, Mia?' the queen would ask, her voice rising with the whisper of a threat.

'I love you above all others, Mother,' Mia would reply — just as she had been taught.

One day, Mia held out a storybook to the queen. 'Mother, there are pictures here of children playing with one another. Are there other children that I might play with?'

The queen's nostrils flared and her eyes turned to ice. 'Why do you need anyone besides your mother?' she asked, her voice trembling with anger. 'Am I not enough for you? Am I not?' She stood over Mia, her hand raised to strike.

Terrified, Mia began to cry. 'Forgive me, Mother, I did not mean it!' she said, stepping back and trying to make herself small.

'Are you sure?' the queen thundered, raising her hand higher, making a fist.

Suddenly the queen's dogs, who had been standing behind her, lunged forward.

'Good dogs!' the queen shouted. 'Get her!'

But the dogs, who had fed on the womb that had nourished Mia, would not hurt her. Instead they leapt up at their mistress, and knocked her down. The queen screamed as one of the dogs went for her throat.

'Help me!' she gasped. 'Mia, help me!'

Mia, trembling, called the dogs to her. Instantly they were at her side, standing beside her protectively.

The queen stood. 'Mia. Do you love me?' she demanded.

'Yes, Mother, I love you above all others,' said Mia, her voice trembling. Beside her, the dogs growled at the queen.

'Are you sure?'

'Yes, Mother, I'm sure.'

'I hope so,' she snarled, 'because this is what happens to those who betray me.' She grabbed the dagger she carried in her sleeve and hacked off the dogs' heads. Then she swept out of the room, leaving Mia to sob over the dead dogs.

Every year on Mia's birthday, the lilac tree outside her window bloomed, and Mia inhaled the sweet scent of the fresh blossoms. The fragrance filled her with sadness and a deep yearning she did not understand. So at every birthday Mia stood by the barred window and wept, and her tears fell and watered the lilac tree, so that it smelled even sweeter the following year.

On her seventh birthday, Mia turned from the window and went to a corner of the room to read. As she passed the queen's dressing table, a shaft of sunlight came through the window, and Mia saw something sparkle and flash on the floor. She bent down to pick it up, and saw that it was a shard of mirrored glass. When she looked at it she saw, not her own face, but the face of a beautiful young woman.

'Lilasette,' said the woman, smiling. 'At last we have found one another, my precious girl.'

Mia was stunned — but she was not frightened. When the woman spoke, something stirred in her heart and soothed her sadness.

'Who are you?' whispered Mia. 'And why do you call me Lilasette?'

'I am Rose, your mother,' the woman in the mirror answered.

'But the queen is my mother,' said Mia, confused.

'No, my sweet girl,' said Rose. 'I am your mother, and I named you Lilasette, for you were born beneath the lilac tree seven years ago today. The queen is your grandmother, and she took you from me. But now that we have found each other, we can find a way to be together always.'

'I cannot leave here,' Lilasette said sadly. 'The queen has locked me in. I am not allowed out without her.'

All at once the door flew open.

'Who are you talking to?' the queen shrieked. 'How did someone get in here?' When she looked down and saw the mirror shard in the girl's hand, she swooped down to grab it. But Lilasette — as she now knew she was — would not release it. The queen tried with all her might to wrench it from her hand, and pulled so hard that when Lilasette finally did let go, the queen's own hand flew backwards, and the glass sank deep into her chest. Shouting with shock and pain, she fell back heavily onto the floor. Blood poured out of the wound, staining her silk dress dark, dark red.

From the mirror shard, Rose's voice implored, 'Run, Lilasette. Run!' Grabbing the mirror, Lilasette fled from the room and out of the palace.

'Go to the lilac tree,' said her mother's voice. 'Wait for me there, and I will come to you.'

Lilasette did as her mother said. But the queen's servants were already pursuing her, and she was frightened.

'Do not be afraid,' said her mother. 'I am with you.'

As the servants approached, the lilac tree bowed down and folded itself over Lilasette. She was wrapped safely in its sweet, soft blossoms, held close to its warm trunk. The servants could not get through the thick leaves and blooms, and they could not harm Lilasette.

And there, within the fragrant branches of the lilac tree, Rose stepped out of the mirror and took her daughter in her arms. For the first time since her mother had held her to her breast, Lilasette felt safe and loved.

Together, Rose and Lilasette emerged from the lilac tree. The mirrored shard, which Lilasette still held in her hand, caught a sunbeam and sent it flashing back towards the servants, so that they could not see the mother and daughter before them.

Happily, hand in hand, Rose and Lilasette walked together into the forest. They lived there in contentment with the wise woman for many, many years. Lilasette learned to speak to the animals and birds, and to heal wounds.

And years later, when Lilasette had a daughter of her own, she planted a lilac tree for her, so that she would always know the sweet scent of safety and love.

The Worm

by

Sarah Hindmarsh

The Worm

It was the third day of March when the young Lord John Lambton took his last fishing trip. The river running through the estate was his alone to fish, and fish he did. In those days he was rarely to be found occupied with anything else, unless it was hunting with his prized pack of fox hounds. He fished most commonly with his friend Alan, of whom his father disapproved most vehemently on account of Alan being the gamekeeper's son and not noble-born. As is often the case with young men, Lord John ignored his father in this, and most other things. That day they were fishing a quiet pool under a copse of silver birch. They caught several fine, fat, trout and counted it a good day for what was likely to be the last fishing day of the season.

Just as they were considering packing up for dinner Lord John felt a small tug on his line.

'Think I've got the last bite Alan.'

The small tug was followed by a larger tug, and Lord John began trying to reel in his line. The rod was almost pulled out of his hands as the creature on the hook tried to escape.

'Help me Alan,' cried Lord John.

Alan rushed to his side and grasped the fishing rod firmly. Even between them they struggled to hold on.

'Cut the line,' said Alan.

'Never, this must be the biggest fish we've ever seen.'

The young lord and his friend battled on until, at last, the line began to slacken.

'It's wore itself out, reel it in.'

So they pulled the line in, inch by torturous inch, until they had reeled it in as far as they could, and all that remained was to land the monster. On the count of three they heaved with all their might, and suddenly, there on the river bank was a writhing, squirming thing that looked like nothing they had ever seen before. Alan and Lord John stared in disbelief. Their nemesis was scarcely five times bigger than the earthworm they had used as bait. How could such a tiny thing have so much strength? They prodded the black worm-like thing with a stick. It emitted a terrible high-pitched shriek, and they jumped back. Two sets of small fins flapped uselessly as the creature wriggled doggedly toward the river. A cavernous opening, that seemed to split its wide, flat head in two, revealed teeth resembling sharp, bony, spines. For reasons even he didn't know Lord John picked up the terrible creature and laid it in the palm of his hand.

'Master,' a rasping voice said. The worm could talk. 'Master help me; put me back in the water.'

Lord John dropped the worm. He was so shocked that he could not move, then Alan spoke up from behind him.

'We ought to be getting back now, John.'

In a flash Lord John swept up the creature and ran to the pond in the gardens below his bedroom window. The worm disappeared under the surface of the pond and both young men thought, and hoped, that that would be the last they would ever have to think about it.

Lord John found his appetite for fishing quite gone. Instead he was plagued by nightmares of the worm; a gnawing hunger invaded his dreams and refused to relent even in his waking hours.

'Meat, I need meat,' a voice in his head repeated over and over again.

In a desperate attempt to be rid of the voice he carried a chicken leg to the pond and threw it in. There was a flash of movement below the surface and a moment later he felt full for the first time in days and a bone, picked clean, floated on the surface of the pond. Lord John discovered that if he repeated this exercise once or twice a day he could appease the phantom hunger. Under the surface of the water he could see the shape of the beast he fed getting larger. He worried about what would happen if the worm became too large for the pond. Over time the worm grew legs and it would meet him on the edge of the pond, greeting him with a delighted hiss.

'Massster, you have come.'

Lord John told his friend Alan how the worm had grown; that it was becoming tame. Alan stayed away from him after that, so John spent his time with the worm, fed it meat from his own plate and gradually began to forget how gruesome it was. The creature was amusing after its own fashion, and its devotion endearing.

When the holy war began Lord John's father sent him to join the king's army, so the worm was left alone. Lord John worried what would become of it. As he rode away he heard a plaintive, wordless cry. He knew it was the worm; a tear threatened to slide down his cheek. Monster though it was; the beast had become as a pet to him. From now on it would have to feed itself. Lord John fought well for the king. He saw many battles in many places, each one a new opportunity to display his bravery. Through it all the worm was with him; a constant reassuring presence at the back of his mind. Occasionally a messenger would get through with a letter from his father. At first the news was no more than mildly troubling.

Dear John,
The gamekeeper thinks a feral dog has been killing our
pheasants. The gamekeeper's son is hunting for it.
All else is well.
Fight bravely.
Father

Lord John had a horrible feeling his worm was at the heart of the problem. In his dreams he could still hear its thoughts. Hunger, then satisfaction, and a terrible rage at being left behind. All these gave way to loneliness, a constant pining for a master the worm believed to be lost to it forever. Lord John felt the anger that drove the beast to hunt; he hoped in vain it was hunting only wild animals.

Over time the letters became more unsettling, so his hope began to fade.

Dear John,

We lost four cows to the beast last week. Nobody can seem to spot the cursed thing. The villagers are concerned for a missing child. They think a lion has escaped from a menagerie. We hope to have the problem addressed before you return home.

Fight bravely.

Father

Still, Lord John could not believe his worm was this terrible beast that was frightening people so. In the quiet times at night he felt its unquestioning devotion to him. Surely it could not love him so fiercely that he could feel it across continents, yet destroy his home at the same time.

When at last the letters reported sightings of the beast John felt his heart sink. There was no doubt that this terror was his worm. The war was almost over; his unit was already heading home by the time he received news of the worm's latest victim.

Dear John,

The beast is getting bigger by the day. Already it is the size of a large horse and it eats all that cross its path. The estate is ruined and the villagers are moving away in their droves. I am afraid there will be precious little for you to return home to unless we find a way to kill it.

It has eaten all those who have tried. I am sorry to say
that the gamekeeper's son you used to be so fond of is the
latest of its victims.
Hurry home John, we need a true warrior to slay the beast.
Fight bravely.
Father

When Lord John arrived on the shores of England once more
he pointed his horse towards his home and rode under a full
moon through the night. He reached the edge of the estate as
the sun was making its first foray above the horizon. He
surveyed the ruin of his former home with a great sadness. He
knew what he must do, although it would break his heart to do
it. Lord John dismounted from his horse and strode boldly on
to the estate.

'Worm!' he called out. 'Worm I am home.'

'Master!' He heard a joyous call and the worm appeared
over the brow of the hill. Lord John grasped his dagger
beneath his cloak.

'Master is home,' the worm cried as it gambolled down the
hill like an excited puppy.

The few remaining villagers emerged from their houses to
see what the commotion was. They screamed to see the great
beast dashing towards their Lord and the horse bolted, his
nostrils flaring wide in terror. Lord John stood his ground.
When the worm reached him it laid its hideous head over his
shoulder, clutching him gently with its fearsome claws. The
worm's joy infused every part of his being, so for a moment
Lord John almost forgot what he had to do. Then,
remembering the wasteland that had been his home he steeled
himself and plunged the dagger through the worm's chest.
Twice, then thrice he stabbed, before the worm had time to
move. On the third stab a tide of warm blood rushed over his

hand. He had pierced the monster's heart, his duty was done.

The worm staggered, then its legs buckled and it fell to the ground. It looked around with sightless eyes, searching for the master it didn't know had betrayed it. The worm struggled to rise, floundering in a pool of its own blood, then it lay quietly, its mouth gaping as it had many years ago when the pool it lay next to was water and not blood.

'Master, I'm hurt,' it said.

'I know, worm.'

Lord John kneeled on the ground and placed his hand beside the wounds he had made. He stroked the worm's unsightly head, felt the confusion in the beast's heart as it slipped away, and knew it was glad he was there in its final moments. He stayed by the worm's side until its grating breaths stopped and no more blood spurted from the holes in its chest. Then, feeling more alone than he remembered it was possible to be, he rose and went to inform his father that the beast was dead.

Paths of Desire

by

Finola Scott

Paths of Desire

All night it cries to her. The sound of the suck and swell tugs at her heart through the wooden planks. She rushes from the hut to see the water. But it is not outside. Instead, a trembling wall of trees blocks the light. Now Ciara remembers what he told her as he loosened her bonds.

'Don't think about escape. Those trees are my fortress. The shore lies far beyond, too far for you. You will never reach it, not on your fresh legs.'

When he hauled his canvas into his hut, she unwrapped in a flood of water. She stared up at him. Smiling, he untied the ropes binding her, and then filled a tin bath. She slipped under the icy water and sighed. It wasn't the sea but she could pretend.

'Truly I'm not bad. There's no need to be fearful. I'll do anything to make you happy, I promise. Now let's make you belong. You'll need a name. I know — Ciara for you came from darkness with wondrous raven hair.'

Combing her long tresses, he told her he wanted her to love him. He promised that they would build a life together. She'd lain in the water, wanting to believe him but still she feared for her future.

So here she is, with only the crying woods for company. Pale morning light shows the hut for what it is — a prison cell. There is no colour or comfort, just a bare scrubbed table, two worn stools and the bed. The tin bath hangs waiting on a nail near the dead fire. Outside in the green clearing round his hut her legs falter but her skin tingles with sea air and the sense of freedom. However, the louring wood frightens her. She feels its power. Ciara is sure hidden creatures watch, eyes unblinking. Though terrified, she's determined to break through this living barrier. She must reach salt water but can see no way. Treetops shiver and sway, but not lushly like her kelp. Laden branches whip her and thorns grasp her legs. She stumbles, but above the smell of dank leaves, she catches brine, the scent of home. She must find a way.

Deeper in, the forest sounds change. Ciara hears not only the creak of wood, now there are cries. She tries to remember what he'd told her. But he warned her of so much.

'Wood creatures,' he whispered baring his teeth, 'foxes, badgers, wolves.'

Deep into the green she realises that although the undergrowth seems dense, there are empty patches. Faint lines wend between trunks. Shafts of sun slip through revealing a large space. In it, a huge tree stands gathering in the sun. Here the sounds are sad, the greenwood whimpers. Her heart shrieks *Turn back!* She won't though, for something calls her, needs her. Heart crashing in her chest, she steels herself. Ciara steps into the light, palms slick with sweat.

In the tree's shade lie three naked forms, skeletal, tangled like a nest of eels. Ciara can't tell if they are scultptures or totems. Her stomach lurches at lank grey hair and puckered faces, shrivelled as bladderwrack. Dark orbs gleam in shrunken sockets. Are these ritual masks? Suddenly one moves. Shocked, she realises they are alive. They are old, but human. Whimpering, they try to shrink back into the gloom, away from her stare. Bile floods her mouth when she realises they are women. She gags at the shock of their faces. Blood-crusted thread locks their mouths shut.

She flees, her feet crushing pungent garlic. Branches snap. Ciara hurtles through the undergrowth, lashing at dense hawthorn. Soft grey doves croon as they soar, but she is not fooled. The wood has shown its power. Relieved, she makes out the shabby hut, suddenly a haven.

On his return, he presents her with a string of shimmering fish.

'For you. I did say I'd make you happy.'

He sighs smoothing her raven hair across his rough sheets. He spins tales of their future, their children scampering in the forest. At his gentle words, she sings to him. But outside the night wood is restless. Misshapen branches twist below the moon. Her dreams are full of bloodied lips, creased flesh hanging on bone.

In the morning Ciara is determined. Those pleading eyes can't be forgotten. She forces her desperate need for the sea to wait. As she battles over twisted roots, she spots white smoke. She can make out shapes moving between the bars of the trees, shuttles in a loom. She hears guttural grunts. A person turns, her eye caught by Ciara's presence. The figure stares and stops dead. Though bedraggled it's definitely a woman, a woman struggling to smile. All Ciara's hesitation vanishes.

'Would you like some?' Ciara offers the battered tin she's brought. 'Goat's milk.'

The spectre nods, gesturing to the rest. Dozens of women, some in rags, stare at her. Most wear makeshift garments woven from bracken. Welcome shines from their faces as they beckon her into their space. On the ground are white shapes protected by shelters. Emaciated women lie on deep leaves beneath sheets of wattle. These are the first to receive the sweet milk. Appalled, Ciara watches wizened throats struggle to swallow. The older mouths seem more open, their stitches looser. Their clawed hands reach out in thanks, their twisted mouths macabre grins. She turns to leave, but some of the women gently still her. Others stroke the crones, murmuring softly. The wizened faces relax as they slip into sleep. Ciara is full of questions but the women shake their heads, it's not the time. For now, she must simply drink their tea with them in quiet.

One bright morn weeks later, she brings a soft mash of fish as well as milk. She kept it back from the evening meal trusting he won't notice. Now that she's grown used to the sound of their tongues clacking in their mouths Ciara feels sure she can follow the women's mutterings. She's eager to learn their histories.

'It was hard, but we were determined to survive. Gradually we taught ourselves to speak again.'

The women sit savouring summer's heat, backs against strong trunks. They nod encouragement to each other as they weave the wattle.

'We all came from a place beyond the woods and shore. We lived easy lives on a fertile plain — all green silk. We thought it Paradise. Our men farmed while we raised the children, all was plentiful. Then... then it turned bad. We grew old, old and useless, according to the men. Our husbands bound us and did this. They silenced us.'

In the shimmering green shade the women softly touch each other's mouths, stroking each wounded lip.

Another takes up their tale. 'When we lived in the village we noticed elders disappearing. I feel bad now for accepting it so easily. At the time I thought they'd died and been taken away. In a sense they had, they'd been brought here, alive. But we didn't know, not then. We soon did, for next it was our turn. Our men began complaining — babies no longer came, our milk dried up. At darkest nightfall in secret our husbands dragged each one of us in turn here, beyond forest paths.

With every visit, Ciara discovers that they refuse to surrender. The women speak to her of the beauty of woodland birds and bright blossom. She rejoices hearing them laugh as they watch aged lips shrink to allow berries on to tongues. Merriment erupts when bright juices run down whiskered chins. She grows addicted to their joy, studying with them as they forage the deep wood teasing out its secrets. She learns which plants are herbs and which make the best teas. They, in their turn, are delighted by her. Stroking Ciara's hair, they wonder over its silky weight and inky sheen. As summer days burn and Ciara grow closer to them, they begin to fret. They question her about her man, warning her against changing moods. She reassures them that he only wants to make her happy. She tells of the songs he's taught her, how he talks about the children they will have.

Ciara is drawn to one woman in particular. From the moment she had turned her dark eyes on Ciara, she had felt safe. With a shock, Ciara realises that the woman reminds her of her mother. The eyes are the same deep pools of brown, soft as dulse. So when that woman explains how the moon rules all their bodies, Ciara pays close attention. Then she understands the preparations her body is making — they are for a child. She isn't prepared though for the row.

That night as she steps out of her bath, he's waiting with the rough fabric, ready to dry her. He nuzzles her silky breasts, caressing her.

Suddenly his face darkens. 'You're bleeding again. I'd hoped... I should have sons. My brothers have lads to share the work.' His voice rises, his face is dark. 'What's wrong with you? When will you give me a child?'

Ciara slips into emptiness. When he's finished, he heaves himself off and rolls into a deep sleep.

Whispering, she cradles her flat belly. 'Please, Mother Moon, let a child take root.'

For days, her arms and mind ache imagining a babe's soft weight. However, when her body responds to the moon's tug once more she feels lost. He turns away, the night she tells him. She fears that this constant hoping and waiting is to be her future. Each night brings his desperate need for a son. And each day Ciara runs to the comfort of the wood women. They talk of their early lives when children were the prize and grind special herbs to ease her difficulty. Obediently she chews cotton grass stems. The women insist that she should trust time, for she's young. Ciara though sees the looks that flash among them.

One evening on returning to the hut, she notices golden tongues of fungus licking the trees. Confetti-like lichen spangles boughs. The next day the women explain that the season is turning. Soon the days will shrink. Ciara realises she'll be alone, imprisoned in his cramped hut by winter dark. She will not be able to spend long happy days with her friends.

In the grimy grey before sunrise, Ciara stares at the room. Dawn is late coming and the hut is chilled. Shadows stripe the walls. Beside her he stirs, shaking in his sleep. He throws a muscled arm over her, trapping her. She shudders remembering the women's look. Over his muttered dreaming, she hears the sighing wood calling, warning, *Run, now, while you can*. By daybreak they're both up, and she smiles a cheerful farewell as he departs as usual. He doesn't know that her smile is for the bundle hidden beneath the bed. For weeks, Ciara has hoarded clothes, scraps of leather and bits of rope. She looks round then kicks the heavy carved crib he's placed beside the bed. According to him it's a family heirloom and he has it ready, waiting for their turn, their boy. Then she's away, running.

In the forest she races along faint paths, marked by fleet-footed ghosts. Before she even reaches the clearing, Ciara hears sobbing. In the women's midst there lies a still form. Sweet jasmine hangs heavy in the air. An elder has died. Solemn women scratch at the earth, their keening hard to her ears. She realises they are carving a grave in a bare patch.

One laughs bitterly, 'This is where we'll all end up, where the men say Thor's hammer struck the earth.'

Ciara presses her bundle on them, her farewell gift, and tells them of her decision.

'We'll miss you, but it's best. Go before winter nips the wood. The year is dying, as we all are. Go — back to the sea and your own folk.'

Again she runs, this time towards the sound, the calling sound. Tangles, branches, thorns can't stop her. At last the rattling boughs become a suck and swell. She smells the wind as salt pricks her skin. Then, she's off the dense path and running over waves of seaweed. She slides across bleached driftwood to clatter onto shells. Periwinkle, oyster and mussel crunch beneath her feet. How could she have forgotten their colour or sheen? Ciara plunges her hands in scooping up fistfuls. Suddenly she has an idea. Eyes flashing, she grips the jewel of them all — a razor shell gleams amber and cream, its edge sharp enough for any barber.

Back she clambers over rocky ridges, struggling through the forest. Heart thudding she picks out the ribbon of smoke, the fire at the heart of the women's home. When she nears, they crowd round puzzled.

'What happened? Why are you back?'

Breathless but grinning, Ciara doesn't answer. Instead, she pushes through to stand over the garland-draped corpse, the shining shell held in triumph. Without saying a word, she reaches down and grasps the dead woman's chin. Her friends press forward shrieking protest. In a flash she brings the jagged edge of the shell down on the cold, pursed mouth. With a few swift slices it's done. The cruel stiches are cut open, pinched lips part. Now throat and tongue are free. Handing the shell to the youngest, Ciara points to where the rippling sea sighs with the wind. She hugs each woman farewell, savouring the soft warmth of their flesh.

She runs over gorges until she reaches shingle. Pebbles mutter welcome. Then she's down deep, released hair swirling in the tide's embrace. Over the surf's song, Ciara hears cries, the best of cries. Her seal family are calling as they've done all summer, their vigil unbroken since he stole her from the dark.

How Women Came to Love Mirrors

by

Hannah Malhotra

How Women Came to Love Mirrors

When a girl got married in the old kingdom of Larberg she gave up her name — her whole name — and nearly everything she had ever been called. Perhaps she should just accept this, we think, for what is a name anyway? Most women of the world part with something of their name when they marry. We remain who we are, do we not? In Larberg, anyway, it was an old practice and it was accepted.

On the eve of her marriage, Anna did not think she would mind. She did not think about it. She was a woman who liked to be pleasing and, besides, she loved Karl. During the wedding ceremony she wrote her name, Anna Larsen, for the last time. Together she and Karl, her hand contained in his, threw the paper into the symbolic fire. Perhaps she felt a flicker of misgiving somewhere deep within, but her hand had only trembled for fear of making a mistake with the letters. Now she was known as Karl's Wife.

A few months into her marriage something unusual happened. Anna was alone in her living room. She had intended to wipe the dust from the mantelpiece but instead she had leant heavily against it, as she was tired after a few hours of housework, and she fell right through the big stone shelf.

For some time Anna lay in the hearth, her skirt in the cold soot, and she tried to understand what had happened. She looked at the mantelpiece for several minutes and then, standing up and ignoring her bruised hip, she ran her hands over the solid stone. She pressed the heavy shelf and then hit it until her hands began to hurt. The mantelpiece was solid, as you would expect it to be. Anna told herself she must have lost her balance and that she was foolish. She could not have fallen through the mantelpiece, what was she thinking? She mimicked a laugh and picked up the dust cloth.

But over the next few months Anna fell through other things. She fell through a sideboard at a dinner party and had to pretend that she had slipped and lost her balance. She upset her husband and a number of other people at the theatre by falling through the balcony of the upper circle. Fortunately she did not break her back, and onlookers believed that she had simply leant too far and toppled over. She even fell through the saddle and body of a horse she had just mounted and it took the groom several minutes to talk himself into disbelieving what he had seen.

Anna knew it was real. She really was falling through things. She decided to talk to Karl about it, to try to explain what was happening.

'What are you talking about?' asked Karl.

'It's true,' Anna insisted. 'I'm falling through things.' Her heart raced and her skin flushed. She felt explosive, somehow. She felt that something unsafe was finding life inside her, something that would not be restrained.

Karl looked at her kindly. He was good-hearted and he loved her very deeply. He wondered if he was failing to understand her, which bothered him because he liked to understand things.

'Are you unhappy?' he asked her quietly. He had heard stories of old aunts of Anna's who had been unhappy and mad.

'I don't think so,' said Anna. 'I am happy with you.' She hid whatever was trying to escape and held out her hand reassuringly.

'I am happy with you too.' He kissed her hair.

That could have been a conclusion, and Karl wished it to be, but Anna could not leave the subject. 'But I am falling through things,' she said. She was surprised by the strength of her voice.

'My darling,' said Karl with just a tiny note of frustration, 'nobody falls through things. It's not possible.'

'I know,' said Anna. 'I know. But I am. It keeps happening. I fall through mantelpieces and chairs. And the balcony, remember? And once, even, a horse...'

'It might feel as though you are falling through things, but you must simply be losing your balance. You can't actually be falling through things. Perhaps I should take you to the doctor?'

Karl was, despite himself, feeling upset. He did not want to think that his wife was unhappy and he did not want her to be saying these things. Anna saw this. She did not want to see the doctor who was even more confident of his opinions than Karl.

'I don't know,' she said. 'Maybe I am just losing my balance. Maybe. It doesn't feel like it though.'

And although Karl loved his wife, he was a man of science and so didn't trust Anna's way of thinking. He decided to assume that her "falling through things" was a hallucination that would soon pass. He was wrong, however. In fact, it got worse, and before long Anna was falling through things so often that someone was bound to find out.

One day, Anna met Hans' Wife when she went to visit her grandmother. Hans' Wife lived next door, with her son and his wife. She was ninety-three and so fragile in appearance that it seemed impossible she could lift a spoon to her mouth let alone walk from her attic room to the parlour two floors below, though this is what she did whenever Anna's grandmother came to visit. She could also talk the devil out of anyone. Her daughter-in-law joked that her mind was polished along with the sideboards. Hans' Wife liked to sit next to Anna's grandmother, and the two seemed to share an understanding despite the fact that Anna's grandmother did not speak. She hadn't uttered a word for a decade and no one could remember what her last sentence had been nor why she had stopped speaking.

Often, on her visits, Anna would sit and hold her grandmother's hand while conducting a conversation with Hans' Wife. They talked of many things including politics and the role of women, and Anna's grandmother would listen keenly. There came a time, though, when Anna's falling through things was really very bad, so she decided to tell the two old women about it. For reasons she couldn't put her finger on Anna sensed that they would not think her ridiculous.

'I'm falling through things,' she said as the three of them sat together by the hearth.

Hans' Wife looked at Anna softly, with deep attention. 'Ah,' she said. 'Ah'.

'It's really bad,' Anna explained. 'I fall through things all the time. I fell through a railing yesterday. It's dangerous.'

Hans' Wife didn't say anything for a while and then she pointed her finger as if to say "stay there". She left the room listing heavily against her stick and looking as if she would surely collapse before reaching the door. Anna held her grandmother's hand and her grandmother looked clearly at her and nodded. Hans' Wife came back with a square shaped piece of glass, the size of a child's palm. She sat down, looked both ways and then turned the glass round. Hans' Wife passed it to Anna. Anna gasped as the glass flung the image of a young woman at her. It was herself.

'It's a reflection!' she exclaimed. There were no mirrors in Larberg in those days, and Anna had only seen herself in water, windows and the polished silver of her mother's best tableware.

'It's called a looking glass, or a mirror,' Hans' Wife said. 'It will stop you disappearing.'

Anna took the looking glass home and made a velvet purse for it. She attached a ribbon and hung the purse around her neck so that she could wear it at all times.

Anna felt better with the mirror around her neck. It didn't help the next time she leant on the dining table and then fell through it, because as usual she had only the faintest tingling sensation in her limbs beforehand. Nevertheless, she took the mirror out as she lay on the floor, and she looked at herself in it. The glimpse showed her to be as three-dimensional as ever, and somewhat flushed in the face, and when she stood back to continue laying the table she felt more solid.

The mirror, secreted under her coats, blouses and dresses, gave Anna renewed confidence. She took it out from under her pillow the moment she woke up and looked into it for reassurance at many times throughout the day. Always it told her the same thing, that she was definitely existing.

Soon Anna discovered that whenever she felt herself beginning to tingle she could draw the mirror up from under her clothes and study her face in it until the tingling subsided. Even the worst tingling sensations subsided if Anna stared at her reflection in the mirror for long enough. Naturally, she was enormously relieved and the possibility of falling through things became less of a worry. In time, she almost forgot that it had happened, and she and Karl loved each other more than ever.

It was when Anna went to visit her grandmother one day, many months and several visits after the one in which she had acquired the mirror, that she thought of the problem of disappearing once more. She was met by the son and daughter-in-law of Hans' Wife, who explained quietly that Hans' Wife had died. Anna felt very sorry. 'How?' she asked, whereupon they told her that the old woman had been found under her bed with a broken neck.

'Of course there was no foul play,' Fredric's Wife said.

'It does seem bizarre though,' said Fredric.

'In some lights it does and in others, not,' said Fredric's Wife.

Anna sat sadly with her grandmother and the old woman patted her arm. A soft smile touched her lips and her eyes seemed to say, 'It was better that you have it.'

Anna ceased crying, but when she went home she did something unorthodox. She stripped her bedroom table of all her husband's writing tools and shoe polish and smoking equipment and she set her mirror there. She examined it thoroughly with a magnifying glass and found that it was in fact plain glass mounted on a different, reflective material. Anna took a knife to the back of the mirror and scratched away at it until some small splinters came apart. She then studied them under her magnifying glass and decided they must be silver.

When her husband came home Anna told him that the mirror was going to stay on the dressing table and that he would have to find a drawer for his things. Karl stared into the mirror, amazed for a moment.

'I have never seen such a true reflection,' he said.

But soon he lost interest and though he'd kept many of his things on the dressing table, he did not object to the mirror. Sometimes he would observe Anna looking at herself in it and consider its effect on her.

'I wonder,' he said one morning as she combed her hair in front of it, 'if perhaps you are becoming addicted to your own image.'

'Every woman should have a mirror,' she said firmly, and that is when she had her idea.

The next day Anna took her mirror to the market and set it up on a table under a sign which read: 'Stop Disappearing – Look In The Mirror.'

'Will this really stop the disappearing?' women asked her cautiously after they had looked.

'Yes,' Anna said over and over again. 'Look into a mirror as many times a day as you wish, and your volume and mass will remain intact.' To other more dubious visitors she would add, 'I think it may work on the mind. The mind which is losing certainty that its body exists is reminded by the reflection in the mirror that its alarm is unjustified and so, in the sense of mind over matter, the body ceases to disappear.' Though, in truth, Anna didn't understand the science of the mirror any better than her customers.

The popularity of Anna's mirror was such that Anna appeared daily in the market and women queued for up to three hours merely to look into it.

One day a merchant passed through the town and seeing the queue of women he thought, *What is being sold here that is so sought after?* He approached Anna and saw the mirror on its table. 'What is it?' he asked her.

'It's a mirror,' Anna told him. 'It is glass laid over silver leaf.'

'Do you sell it?' he asked.

'No,' replied Anna. 'It is the only one.'

The merchant went home and thought about the mirror. After dinner he asked his wife a question. 'Have you seen this mirror in the market?'

The merchant's wife blushed and tried to hide her face. 'Yes,' she said, 'I have seen a little of it.'

'Is it really true that all women want to see themselves in it?'

'There are women who wait in the market from five in the morning, though Karl's Wife does not come until eight, because they want to look in the mirror so much,' the merchant's wife told her husband. 'And there are women who forget to go home and cook dinners for their husbands because they are still waiting to see themselves in the mirror.'

The following day the merchant ordered enough glass and silver leaf to make mirrors for all the women in Larberg. He too set up a stall in the market and at it he sold, for the price of a week's meals, small gleaming mirrors. Within three days he had sold his entire stock and there was not one woman who had the money to afford one who did not have a mirror somewhere in her house or in a bag close to her body. Presently the merchant moved away from Larberg to sell mirrors to women in other parts of the continent.

Anna took her own mirror home and put it back on the dressing table.

'I think,' she said to her husband that night, 'that soon there will not be a woman anywhere in the world who does not begin and end the day by looking at herself in a mirror.'

Karl looked wonderingly at her but Anna smiled at her reflection because she knew she was right.

Perhaps she dreamed of a day when women would not need the mirrors. Perhaps she did.

Fox Fires

by

Jane Wright

Fox Fires

Up in the far, far north, where the days are short and the nights are long, a beautiful white fox lived in the bleak white world. Fox was young, little more than a cub, and she was a happy soul, impish and joyful. When she wasn't out hunting for food or sleeping the short days away in her den, she liked to frolic around in the snow. Fox would run and pounce and dance, kicking up her paws and leaving deep trails and patterns behind her.

Late one afternoon, when darkness had already fallen and the landscape was shining silver in the light of the moon, Fox went out to hunt. After she had filled her belly she decided it was time to play. As she pranced around in a particularly deep snow drift she began swishing her tail, sweeping gusts of snow up into the air. The moon was full, strong and bright, and as the snow arced higher and higher into the sky, the moonlight caught it and it began to glow beautiful colours; green and blue and pink and white. Lighter than feathers, the flakes hung in the air and danced there like a shimmering curtain of light. Fox stood looking up, surveying her work, and she smiled widely. The lights filled her with joy and she sat watching them as they glittered and sparked and moved on the air, always shifting and undulating like a wave. When she saw they were beginning to fade Fox started to swish again, sending more glittering flakes up into the air to replenish the colours.

Down in the village, Girl was giving birth. She was also young and little more than a cub herself. It was her first child, fathered by a man who had left as soon as he knew, and the pregnancy had been hard and difficult. Now it was almost over and she had been labouring for hours but something was terribly wrong; she could feel it deep in her belly and deep in her soul. Women crowded around her, their warm, clammy hands slick with her blood, prodding and poking at her skin, wiping the sweat from her brow and grasping her hands as she moaned and cried. Mother urged Girl to push a little more as it was so close, so Girl mustered the last dregs of her strength and pushed and pushed and screamed and screamed, and a small, limp, breathless body fell from her womb and slithered silently into the world.

Mother laid the lifeless form on her breast so that Girl could say hello and goodbye to Daughter. The women stepped back and melted into the shadows of the cottage as Girl looked at her tiny daughter and thought how unexpectedly peaceful she looked after the hours of agony they had both just endured; how unexpectedly peaceful and how utterly beautiful. Pain mingled with despair and a sudden unyielding wave of love, and she kissed Daughter gently, as tears dripped from her cheek onto the tiny child's.

The room was hot and sticky and it smelled of grief and death, so Mother went to the window. She pulled back the heavy material obscuring the room from the world outside and opened the window to let some air, and some life, into the room. As she did so she saw a curtain of beautiful coloured lights hanging in the sky to the north and she gasped. She stood watching for a moment in both awe and fear and then, pushing the material back as far as it would go, she turned back to the room full of sombre women and said, 'Look. It's Daughter.' And with that, she took the tiny body from Girl's sweat-drenched breast and clutching fingers, and went outside with her.

Night after night Fox played happily, sweeping more and more snow up into the air with her tail; filling more of the sky and making the colours glow brighter and brighter.

And night after night, Girl sat outside in the freezing darkness, gazing up at Daughter's soul as it burned brighter and brighter, grieving for the child that never even took a single breath.

Fox was so excited by what she had created that she wanted to share her joy with others. One night, after making her most beautiful, colourful display yet, she decided to go in search of some new friends so she could show them what she had done. She walked for a while and at last she wandered down into the village. She expected to see people standing outside and looking up at her work, admiring it, but as she walked through the cluster of houses she saw only Girl, sitting alone in her vigil. Fox's pride was slightly dented but she could see that Girl was full of grief so she padded over to her and asked her what was wrong. Girl turned her tear-stained face to Fox and was moved by the softness in the dark eyes looking back at her.

'I lost my daughter,' she said simply. 'She never took a single breath in this world and it feels as though my heart is splitting in two.'

Fox sat down next to her and rested her nose on her paws. She was lost for words as she had never before seen pain like that written in the face of a human, but eventually she said, 'I'm so very sorry. I cannot imagine how that feels.' Then she asked, 'But why do you sit out here, where it's freezing cold, staring up at the lights in the sky?'

'Because,' said Girl, 'those lights appeared for the first time as her soul left this place, and I know that it's her up there, watching over us. So I sit out here so that I can feel closer to her, and hope that one day I'll be able to touch her again.'

'Oh,' Fox said quietly. Suddenly she didn't feel proud of what she'd done.

'I never even got to tell her her name,' Girl continued, fresh tears falling from her eyes. 'I wish so much that I could speak to her, just once.'

135

Girl's story made Fox realise that her wondrous creation had imprisoned Girl in her grief. She looked up at the shimmering colours that were beginning to fade and saw the fear in Girl's face as she thought her daughter was leaving her yet again. Fox wanted to help Girl more than anything and she suddenly had an idea.

As the last of the colours faded, and Girl choked back a sob, Fox said, 'You can bring her back. If you sit here and whistle to her, Daughter will hear you and she will know you're still here. And if you keep whistling she will come closer and closer, and maybe she will come close enough for you to be able to whisper a message to her. You might finally be able to tell her her name.'

Girl's eyes widened and for the first time since Daughter had gone, the grief in them was replaced with hope. Fox jumped up as Girl turned her face to the skies and began to whistle, and she trotted into the dark shadows behind some houses. Finding the deepest, purest drift of snow that she could, Fox began to work. As Girl whistled, Fox kicked and swept and danced, her paws and her tail sweeping wave after wave of snow into the sky above Girl. As the lights became brighter and closer, Girl's whistling became stronger and more musical, and Fox kept sweeping and sweeping until the lights hung all around Girl and she could reach out and almost touch them. Eventually Girl stopped whistling and instead Fox could hear her murmuring into the night. Fox kept on swishing as long as Girl kept on whispering, and only when she finally fell silent did Fox stop her kicking and go back to Girl. Lighter than feathers, the flakes still hung in the air, shimmering their beautiful colours, swirling and undulating, and as Fox approached Girl, she heard her say, 'Daughter, I love you.'

Tired out from her exertions but feeling more love in her heart than she had ever known before, Fox curled up next to

Girl and closed her eyes. As she lay there, she felt a warm hand come to rest on her back, and soft gentle fingers curled and buried themselves into her fur.

'Thank you,' Girl whispered.

And Fox was proud of her creation once more. As they sat together, Girl's hand rose up and down with Fox's breathing and Fox suddenly felt more loved than she could possibly have dreamed of. As she lay with her eyes closed and Girl's hand on her back she smiled to herself, as she knew then that she was home.

Solstice

by

Deborah Osborne

Solstice

The Holly King's hall is full of light and noise. Candle wax drips onto the iron chandelier hanging high above the raised dais. The fires blaze. Fast, frantic music rolls through the crowd, as each man lifts his voice, in order to chase away the shadows of the longest night.

My lord, the Holly King, sits at the raised table, feasting himself into a stupor. Reflected flames dance across his crown, flickering over the polished surface, turning it into a circle of molten gold. His laugh is deep, and it reminds me that I did love him once.

Part of me still loves him. But tonight, the darkness outside stretches so far ahead and behind me that I feel restless. My chest tightens, and the celebration is unsatisfying.

Scarlet rests his head in my lap, brown eyes lifting to look at me, and his tail thumps the floorboards in the contentment only a dog can find. John and Tuck have followed him. John lays his mighty head on paws the size of dinner plates. Tuck chews on a marrow bone. They've been outside in the snow. Fine crystals have dampened their fur. I too crave the freshness of ice cold air, the promise of an adventure in the raw emptiness of a midnight forest.

The feast surges around me in all its brightness and heat. I sit quietly, fingers buried in Scarlet's ruff, afraid to move. I'm afraid to stay, and afraid to go.

My lord is the last to succumb to drink. 'I do love you,' he murmurs.

'I know.' I touch his cheek and his skin feels dry, like dead leaves.

He slides into sleep. The crown tips from his head as he slumps forward over the table. His hair is greyer now. In sleep he looks tender, with delicate eyelids and lips. I do not wish to leave him, but the darkness is pressing against the window glass. It seeps beneath the doors. Ignoring it won't banish it. Lighting another torch will only lengthen the shadows.

Low down in my belly excitement wiggles free, closely followed by fear. Scarlet whines as I stand, dislodging his head from my knee.

It is time. Tonight, the year is poised to change.

I pull on my cloak. Scarlet watches with dark, questioning eyes. John lifts his head, ears perked.

Before I can change my mind, I am off the dais. All through the great hall, men are sprawled together in the straw. I weave through them on the balls of my feet, avoiding fingers.

Scarlet whines, low and needy. My heart lurches. One of the men-at-arms grumbles as I step over him, but doesn't awake.

At a whispered command, Scarlet's rump hits the floor, but he looks at me reproachfully. He wants me to stay. I want to stay. The castle is safe and warm, but that is the problem. It's easier for them because as dogs they do not remember that it is too safe, too warm. If I remain here we will continue on in a stupor, winter will reign forever. The sun will not rise.

One of the large iron-studded doors is cracked open, and cold, pale moonlight whispers through to dance patterns on the floor. No one stirs as I reach hesitantly for the gap. I take a breath, then slip outside and into freedom.

The first step is magic. The snow sinks beneath my boot with a satisfying crunch. Air stings my cheeks and cools my lungs. I've yearned for this even as I've feared it. I want to remember how to lie beneath the stars, in my lover's arms, and not know what the next day will bring. I miss being that woman, even as her recklessness scares me.

I run through the palisade, over the bridge where the moat is frozen, and through the sleeping fields until I stand on the edge of the forest.

The trees are laced with silver. They curl their spindly fingers towards me, twirling my breath around their points and drawing me forward. They are knit so tight I cannot see through them, but I can hear them creak beneath the weight of the snow. I know that in the forest you become what is needed. In the forest an outlaw can become a hero, or he can share the face of a god. I pull back my skirt, extend my leg, and place my foot firmly in the shadows.

From behind the high palisade, the dogs howl. Their voices flow together, splitting the hushed night. Scarlet has betrayed me. Horses will be woken, armour put on. My lord will be coming for me. I duck beneath the closest branches and flee. The ground dips and sways beneath my feet. The only noises are my breath and the crackle of snow. My body is soft and weak after a winter hidden safe inside, and the dogs hunger for the chase. I clamber over a fallen birch tree, my hands and knees slipping on the ice. The air constricts my chest. The soft skin of my throat is on fire with the effort, but I am close to the forest's heart.

The dogs communicate with short, staccato barks. They are gaining.

At the centre of the forest is a hill. The ground veers upwards and I scrabble on hands and the tips of my toes. The dogs' warm breath heats my ankles as I tumble onto the crest of the hill.

I seize a dead branch, swinging hard as Scarlet leaps. It is a weak move, but he is knocked aside and rolls on the ground. I clamber to my feet, and run. Gasping, reaching for the nearest oak tree. The muscles of my arms burn as I pull myself up. Tuck's teeth snap at my toes. John raises to his hind legs, neck straining.

I push myself back against the trunk. My breath is mist, my hair is savage. The dogs bare their teeth at me. Their ears lie flat, and they pace. Waiting. They know that their master is near.

My lord rides into the clearing. The grey charger puffs twin jets of steam, and its large hooves kick up a spray of ice. His eyes, the shocking evergreen of holly leaves, are sad. 'I knew you would run.' Resignation sits in the roughness of his voice and the slump of his shoulders.

I want to comfort him, but from the top of the hill I can see beyond the forest to the horizon. It is still dark, and will remain so until this night's work is done.

My lord dismounts. The dogs slink back, their ears flat against their scalps. I look around the clearing at the silent oaks and the still holly bushes. When my lord offers me his hand, I take it.

He is still strong enough to lift me down from the tree. I could let him put me onto his horse and carry me away back to his castle. Part of me still wants the security of those high stone walls, but I have already slept too long, and too deep.

The air tremors as someone else walks into the clearing. A boy with eyes as green as sun-dappled oak leaves rests his shoulder against a nearby trunk. Dark brown hair falls into his eyes. He eats a winter apple.

'Shall I kill him for you, my lady?' He smiles.

My lord roars his challenge. I'm thrown down into the snow as he draws his broadsword free with a hiss of cold air. The dogs crowd round me, and I have to fight through a swirl of muzzle to see what happens next.

The boy has nothing but an iron-bound staff. Neither he nor my lord moves. They have done this too many times to rush now.

I have watched too many times, but still my fists clench.

The first clash of iron on wood sends ripples through the forest.

My lord has grown weak, but he has more experience. The boy falls. The staff bursts from his fingers. My lord stands over him, sword raised. The dogs howl. The boy twists, his foot strikes out and my lord tumbles to the ground. The boy picks up his broken staff and stands above him, poised to smash in his skull.

I don't want it to end like this, even though end it must. Still, I am a forest maid now. I am brave again.

I break free of the dogs, and throw myself across my lord's chest.

'Marian?' The boy lifts an eyebrow at me, but he backs down beneath the ferocity of my glare.

My lord's hands find my hair, cradling my head against his neck. His lips are as cold as I remember them, and his eyes shine.

'I gave you everything I could.' My lord says, 'I kept you safe. I loved you.'

His hair is pure white now, and his shoulders are thin. The crown has already fallen from his head.

I touch his face. 'You have done all that, but it is not enough.'

'It is never enough.'

'No.' I caress his jaw, one last time. Then I pull his dagger from his waist. He smiles as I slip the blade beneath his arm, high and clean.

The heat of his blood coating my hand is a shock, but I stay with him until the end. When his life is gone, I wipe my hands in the snow. The boy helps me to my feet, and we stand by my lord's body, fingers entwined, as his skin hardens, each age line melting into bark. He sends out roots, and sharp holly leaves unfurl from his fingers.

The dogs stumble forward, legs stretching until they become men. Scarlet shakes off the last of his fur. He throws back his head and laughs at the clear morning sky. Tuck lifts his skirts and dances. The only betrayal of John's pleasure is the slight curl of his lip. There is an exuberant, May Day feel to the air. But summer is a long way off. There is work to do. I clean my lord's blade on my skirt and strap it to my thigh.

The crown is entwined in the holly leaves, and they scratch as I twist it free. The boy bows his head, and I think that he will wear the crown well. Although he is not so much of a boy now. He stands taller. His smile has lost its carefree cheek. Already his merry eyes can see the year unfurling ahead of him. Still, he spins me round, and his shout of joy sends the crows cawing from the trees.

We have no secrets from each other and he knows that his reign is not eternal. He knows he will also grow old. He knows that when the sun is fat and high, I will grow restless. When the time comes, he knows, I will kill him too.

For the moment, the whole summer lies ahead of us, and beyond the edge of the forest, the sun begins to rise.

Rêve/Revival

by

Elizabeth Hopkinson

Rêve/Revival

Carabosse

Only when she saw her reflection in the mirrored hall did she realise how much she had aged. The once-golden leaves of her hair were withered to a brittle brown. Cobwebs traced lines across her face; a black beetle clung to her lower lip. She watched the royal party shrink from her, crossing themselves, clutching at their breasts and their stolen jewels.

'Murderers!'

Her voice came out as hoarse as that of the raven mourning its ancient roost.

'Despoilers of the forest! Slayers of deer and boar!'

She pointed a finger — a talon now — at the minstrels' gallery, bedecked to bristling with antlers, crossbows, muskets. The young duke prided himself on single-handedly ridding the forests of the Steinburg of its bears. Even now, his fingers shone with plundered amber, and the tables of the christening feast groaned with salmon, partridge, swan, hare. Now he dared to speak of progress. Of mines and factories. Of canals cutting gashes across the countryside. Her pointing finger trembled.

'I curse you, Duke Florestan! A life for a life. A child for a child.' Her gaze turned on the babe in the cradle, stiff with lace and swaddling. 'Let your beloved daughter grow. Let her become the light of your eyes, the joy of your heart. Then let her be struck down on the brink of womanhood.'

She turned on the duke, eyes burning.

'And feel your heart being torn from your living breast.'

Aurora

Only that morning, she had received four suitors.

'Alliance is crucial,' her father had insisted. 'Bonaparte

devours the lands like a ravening boar. We can no longer rely upon the Emperor's protection. Together, the small states will be stronger. You must do your duty, Aurora. The Steinburg depends on you.'

The choice had been on her mind for months. Yet when the old fairy stepped out from behind the dressing screen, she couldn't say she was surprised. The face was more haggard than the one she saw in her dreams; the leaves of the hair were mere skeletons, the figure a frail twig.

'Your time has ended.'

The fairy's voice was a hiss of reeds in the wind. Aurora took her by the elbow and guided her towards a chaise-longue. The faint tug of resistance lasted only a moment.

'You are here to kill me,' Aurora said. 'To bring an end to my father's line. Do you honestly believe that will save the forest? That Bonaparte will not fell its oaks to build his ships? That he and the Emperor will not carve up the land between them, to do with as they please?'

The fairy gave a sigh, filling the room with the odour of rotting logs.

'Do you not have a better plan than that?' said Aurora.

Their eyes met.

Carabosse

For the first ten years, she slept with the rest of them. Raising the barrier of enchantment around the Steinburg had taken the last of her strength. She was tired, so tired. Tired of anger, tired of the fight, tired of the sorrow that gnawed away at her soul. It was a comfort to feel cobwebs spin softly on her shoulders, to smell the growing scents of nettle and bramble, even in sleep.

The spiders came first. And after them, the beetles and moths, whirring small wings around the silver cruets and wax fruit.

Then came the badgers, nudging, nosing. The skittering feet of mice. Squirrels clambering up the pillars of the great hall, twisting foot by foot about the staircase. Agile weasels leaping in and out the leaves.

By the time she woke, there was a copper beech sprouting through the floorboards of the library. The eleventh generation of wood warblers had taken roost among the hunting trophies. By the time she felt strong enough to dance once more, the copper branches shimmered with the murmuration of starlings.

By the time the prince arrived, the Steinburg was a wilderness.

Florimund

The world would never go back to the way it had been. Every day he'd read the telegrams. Men drowning in mud. Horses screaming. And nearer to home, small states caught between the Tsar and the Kaiser. The pincers tightening and tightening until... Well, it was inevitable that something was going to snap.

He'd wanted to do so much for his people. Education, better housing, votes for women. But the mob had got louder, more extreme. His mother had survived a mere two months in exile, his father even less. They'd taken the Emperor's offer of refuge, but now the Imperial throne had fallen too, and Florimund was weary. He wished there was somewhere he could go, away from this terrible new century. Disappear. Bury the shame and the sorrow.

He had discovered the castle by accident. After days of riding, riding, not even knowing where he meant to go. Beneath the moss and the fungus, the furniture was Napoleonic, of a sort that his great-grandfather might have used. He wanted to laugh at the innocence of a time when men marched to the tune of drum and trumpet, and attended balls on the eve of battle. Weeping, he let mice run over his hands. He lay in the ballroom on a great mattress of rosebay willowherb, laughing and sobbing alternately.

The fairy didn't come to him until the third week. By that time, he'd already found the people, decided they weren't waxworks, pressed his head against their chests to hear their gentle breathing. The girl was beautiful — he acknowledged that — but he envied her more than he desired her. The peacefulness of her seclusion. Her unconscious affinity with the butterflies that landed on her lashes, the squirrels that chased in and out of her long, long hair. What happened when nations awoke but battle and bloodshed? Better to be guilty of nothing more than spending your life in a fantastical dream.

When the fairy arrived, she was breathtaking. Hair the gold of beech leaves in autumn. Eyes of glowing amber. The sprinkling of fur on the tips of her ears was soft, like that of the pet rabbit he had had as a boy.

'I have waited long for the right man to rule my forest.'

Her voice was like the bubbling of a mountain spring. Florimund held out his hand.

'You have found him.'

Carabosse

The Napoleonic furniture and medieval crossbows had long since crumbled away, slowly digested by moss and ivy. Doe grazed in the ballroom. Furry-eared children played under the beech trees in the library. It had been a long time since Carabosse had visited the Steinburg. The roses grew wild over Florimund's grave in the forest. His children had passed away too, but his grandchildren lived longer, the fairy strain growing stronger with each new alliance. But extinguishing the human line was a dream of yesterday. She had pledged to honour her word. It was time.

Taking her great-great-grandson by the hand, she led him to the chamber where Aurora lay, entombed in brambles and gorse. Together, they cut a way through, hands exposed to the stab of thorns, accepting the pain. When the face was finally revealed, Carabosse saw the young fey-man smile, the feathers round his cheekbones trembling.

'Your bride,' Carabosse said. 'Love her well.'

The fey-man bent to kiss the sleeping beauty.

Little Lost Soul

by

Marija Smits

Little Lost Soul

*

The Forest of Miracles
for David

There is a forest deep in Russia:
the Forest of Miracles.
Tall pines stretch limbs,
oaks straddle leaf-mould.

The forest is forbidden,
and men may forage only briefly there,
muffled in masks, their Geiger counters bleeping,
signalling to each other through antique silence.

Now strange shapes sprout;
the wrong leaves and convoluted growths
whisper shady secrets.
The crunch of pine needles
is deadly — and the toadstools.

ANGELA TOPPING

*

When Dr Yelena Ivanovna Belova first opened the door to the young woman she did not notice the bruises on either side of the woman's neck. It was only when she was partway through explaining that all her counselling hours were assigned that she saw them brooding, like two ugly amethysts, under the striplights of the corridor.

Yelena, who had spent the day listening to the problems of both Subordians and Direktors, was tired and wanted nothing more than to get back to her quarters, but the bruises were too distressing to ignore; in the past five years since she'd been here in the Chernobyl Robotics Facility nobody had ever come to her with any signs of physical abuse. She invited the woman into her office.

'I know it's late,' began the young woman, 'but I'm new here and...' She put her hands to her neck.

'A man?' asked Yelena.

The woman nodded.

'One of the Subordians?'

Unexpectedly, the woman shook her head.

Yelena tried to mask her alarm and then indicated that the woman should take a seat. She then walked to the AI interface at the side of her desk and began to speak to it.

'But this is confidential, *Da?*' said the woman, looking at the screen, her eyes fearful.

'Of course. The AI is never on when I'm in a session. But I do need to log this meeting.'

The woman seemed to shrink in her seat, like a child who has nowhere to conceal herself in a game of hide-and-seek, but then she jumped to her feet and made for the door, saying that this maybe wasn't a good idea.

Yelena quickly came to her side and put a gentle hand on her arm. 'You're frightened, I know. I'm sorry. I can log this later. Let's just sit, and talk, if you want to. The AI will be off, I promise.'

The young woman returned to her seat and Yelena told the AI to shut itself down. She then made herself comfortable in her own seat and began the process of listening to the young woman who refused to say anything about the person who had given her the bruises, though she was quick to explain the why of the matter... *Because I am a monster.*

After the young woman had left, Yelena spent some time looking at her new patient's files. Her name was Natalya Mikhailovna Bochkaryova, and she was twenty-two, just out of Moscow State University. Her hair, which was so fair it was almost white, was a trait inherited from her mother, who had died when Natalya was very young. There was little resemblance to her father who was, as Yelena had already guessed, an alcoholic who had beaten her. She had done well in her studies, although it was often said that she lacked focus. That would probably explain why she'd managed to lose her ID pass in the first week of being in the facility. It had been recorded as "showing a distinct lack of attention". Yelena smiled wryly at the thought of those ridiculous paper passes. Considering that security was of paramount importance, as they were continuously told, the Direktors were still enamoured of their bits of paper and their human guards, who seemed like relics of a bygone era. The guards, forbidden the use of anything more technologically advanced than a biro, spent most of their days playing cards and drinking smuggled-in vodka.

On paper, as it were, Yelena wouldn't have considered Natalya to be of psychological interest; she would have categorised her as yet another little lost soul, who believed that her worth could only be measured by others. That to please (and be pleasing) was her only role in life. But in the flesh... well, she was far more interesting than the other Subordians. They were mostly homesick, or in love with someone who didn't love them. The Direktors' problems were more varied, but equally dull. They agitated over their relationships with their spouses. Were they still *loved?* Were they still *in* love? Should they take a lover? And of course they fretted about their careers. The only Direktor who didn't have these problems was Viktor Yudovich Ozimov, who they all knew as the Father, since he was the Direktor of New Robotics. He, as Yelena had often noted, was more in love with his robots than with anyone or anything else. It was strange, really; considering that most of them either built or worked with faceless plastic robots day in and day out in a lead-lined building just outside the exclusion zone of Chernobyl, and yet none of them seemed to have any concerns about the unique nature of the facility. There had been one Subordian though, a young man, whose dreams had plagued him throughout his two-year stay. He had dreamt of flesh being seared by white-hot circuits and radioactivity seeping out of the trees and into the cracks of the building. He had been an anomaly. Until now. Now there was Natalya and her constant assertion that she was a monster.

'As you don't wish to speak of your assailant, let us explore this belief of yours. That you are a monster,' offered Yelena at their next session.

Natalya said nothing and sat, impassive.

'You think of yourself as a monster and yet all I see before me is an intelligent young woman. In fact, you rather look like myself when I was young. Though that was many, many years ago.'

Natalya smiled.

'Did he call you a monster, when he gave you the bruises?'

Natalya bowed her head and put her hands to her eyes. A sob left her throat. She then raised her head and Yelena could see a perfect sparkling tear on each cheek.

'But he sometimes says kind things. He calls me his *matryoshka*, his perfect doll. But he always ends by telling me that I must know my place. That I must not let thoughts of superiority come into my mind. And then...'

'I see,' said Yelena, considering each of the male Direktors. Which one of them was hurting her?

'And you think he is right? That you are a monster?'

Natalya slowly nodded her head.

'You are very ready to believe what he says. Have others said this to you?'

Natalya's eyelids fluttered and then she said, 'Yes. Although to my face my father calls me his clever girl, behind my back he calls me a monster.'

'And what of your mother?' said Yelena, wording her questions carefully.

'I have no mother.'

Yelena took a deep breath. 'You have learnt, from an early age, that you are a monstrous person, a nobody, a nothing, and so you accept this new man, although he is dominating and violent because it is what you expect. It is your normal. But I am here to tell you that it isn't normal, do you understand? You are not a monster, and you have every right to live free from harm. Do you see? To preserve your soul, your very essence, you must take control of your fate.'

Yelena sat back in her chair and then glanced at the clock. 'I'm sorry,' she said, sighing, 'but today's session is at an end. We've overrun, actually.'

Natalya stood up and approached Yelena. She laid her hand on Yelena's arm and thanked her.

'What you just said.' She paused. 'I have dreamt of someone being kind enough to say those words to me.'

Yelena smiled as Natalya said goodbye and then left her office. She allowed herself the brief glow of satisfaction that came from helping another woman take her first steps to empowerment, for she knew from experience that often, satisfaction was followed by disappointment. These women, the little lost souls, needed support and encouragement. But where would Natalya receive these things in the facility? From the other Subordians, who knew nothing beyond their endless work or drunken flings? Or the faceless robots who said nothing more than *Privyet?* And she certainly wouldn't get it from the Direktors. When Yelena had raised her concerns with the other Direktors about the possibility of a case that involved abuse she had been dismissed with a *Nothing like that could happen here.* Yelena sighed, logged their meeting and then put Natalya out of her mind.

It was a fortnight later, in the Kantina, when Yelena next saw Natalya. Yelena, sat with the other Direktors, looked up from the bowl of borscht she'd just been served by one of the robots and suddenly noticed her at the end of one of the tables assigned to the Subordians. She seemed different, more substantial, somehow; more ruddy and round-cheeked than she remembered her being. And she looked happy. Yelena smiled.

Natalya, suddenly aware that she was being studied, looked at Yelena and returned her smile; though Yelena noticed that there was confusion in Natalya's eyes. This wasn't uncommon. Some of her patients didn't like to admit that they'd been speaking with the facility's counsellor. Yelena turned back to her soup and took another spoonful as Vladimir Afanasy Arkonovich, the Direktor of Security and Viktor Yudovich Ozimov, the Father, joined her. Vladimir sat down heavily and then picked up a bread roll, which he proceeded to butter in a slapdash fashion.

'Yelena,' was all he offered as a greeting.

'You seem...' Yelena studied his sweat-damp face and beady eyes. 'Perturbed.'

Vladimir gripped his knife even tighter and then thumped the handle on the table.

'Yes, I am perturbed.'

'Work problems?'

'Work problems... women problems. It's all the same to me.'

Yelena glanced at his fat hands before returning to her borscht, but she failed to see anything incriminating about them.

'Well, if you ever need to talk to someone...'

Vladmir ignored her, as he always did — he could not bear the fact that she had the power to declare him mentally unfit for work — and instead began to admonish the Father about his new vanity project.

It had been a particularly trying day for Yelena. She was just about to leave her office when Natalya burst in; she was clutching her left arm, which was covered in blood.

'My God!' Yelena cried. She rushed to where the first aid kit was kept and pulled out some bandages. 'How did this happen?'

'I finally told him what you said. And that I'd had enough of him calling me a monster. He picked up a knife. I tried to push him away, but...'

'Natalya, you must tell me who did this.'

Natalya shook her head. 'I can't.' Two tears appeared on her cheeks. 'Not here. He might be listening.'

Yelena knew what she had to do. It would require bribery, since Subordians were forbidden from leaving the facility, but it could be done.

'Very well. Follow me, and don't say a thing.'

Twenty minutes later, Yelena, now bereft of two bottles of vodka, walked out of the facility with Natalya. They began to laugh as they took deep breaths of fresh air.

'Isn't it wonderful?' said Natalya as they reached the edge of the forest. In the distance they could see the exclusion zone, but beyond the 'Keep Outs' was the glorious, setting sun.

They walked into the forest and after a few minutes of silence, Yelena told Natalya that she thought she knew who was hurting her. She put her arm around her. 'I can make this stop.'

There was a sudden shout. 'Yelena!'

They both froze and then Natalya ran, into the dark heart of the forest; Yelena, caught between hunter and hunted, didn't know what to do.

'Yelena!' It was Vladimir.

Yelena walked out of the forest, into the fast-disappearing light and saw something she wasn't expecting: someone who looked very much like Natalya standing next to Vladimir.

'Natalya?' she said uncertainly.

'Where did it go?' asked Vladimir. 'The monster? Did it go towards the exclusion zone?'

Yelena, her mind reeling, nodded and Vladimir cried out in anger, his fists suddenly aloft.

'But I don't understand,' said Yelena, looking at the young woman in front of her. It was then that she noticed that the woman's arm was unhurt. 'Who are you?'

'This is the real Natalya,' interjected Vladimir. 'And the Natalya who you've been giving ideas to is the Father's latest monstrosity — a devious robot, with skin and a face and a twisted sense of its own importance, who realized that its physical similarity to this new Subordian was its way out of here. Once it had convinced you to get it out. I was trying to get it destroyed. You fool, Yelena. You have set free the most expensive, thinking doll ever built. And we can't follow it into the exclusion zone and we can't track it since it's destroyed its tracking device.'

Yelena thought of Natalya's wound and the bruises, and the lies. But had they all been lies...?

She turned around and walked to the forest's edge and called Natalya's name, but there was no response. And she breathed deep the pine-scented air as shame and anger and pride and fear stormed through her expansive human soul.

Trash Into Cash

by

Becky Tipper

Trash Into Cash

There was once a tall and teetering city perched on a tiny island; a city where the buildings reached so high that they tickled the heavens, and which at night glittered with lights that rivalled the stars themselves.

Our tale, however, begins in the tumbledown edges of this city, in a neighbourhood where the poorest people lived and where the city relegated the things it didn't wish to see or think about. In this cluttered, unpretty place dwelled a merchant who made his living from the waste of the world.

The merchant dealt in metals, gathering the discarded scraps that the city had cast off and melting them down so that they might be made into new, shining items for the city people (who hungered always for new, shining items).

The scrap-merchant's yard was piled with metal in every conceivable form: old cars, kitchen appliances, gates and railings, drinks cans, pieces of unidentifiable machinery. Some was crushed already into square bales, and some waited in tangled, rusting piles to be sorted. In the trailer that served as the merchant's office were sad little tubs of jewellery — wedding rings exchanged by long-departed spouses, fragments of gold chains, and empty silver lockets that once held a wisp of some beloved's hair.

At the entrance to his yard, a flashing neon sign announced to passers-by, who might wish to rid themselves of superfluous metal, that here they could convert their 'trash into cash'. A bold claim indeed.

The merchant lived with his daughter, a girl almost old enough to be considered a woman. The merchant's wife (the girl's mother) had died many years ago, so that the girl had now only the faintest memories of her and could not even quite recall her mother's face.

Now, the merchant was not a bad or cruel man. But he was vain and boastful and liked to drink, which frequently amounts to the same thing. However, the girl was patient and gentle, and she loved her father in spite of his many faults and for the most part they lived together quite happily.

One day, late in the afternoon, a wealthy businessman came from the city. The businessman had a car he wished to sell to the merchant — a car which had been very expensive and which the businessman had driven carelessly and had managed to wreck. The businessman didn't need the money that the merchant offered him for the vehicle — he had plenty of that already (and he even owned many other cars) but he was an avaricious man, unable to pass up an opportunity to acquire a little more of anything.

After they had agreed on a sum for the unfortunate car, they shook hands and the merchant offered the businessman a beer — a drink to seal the deal, he said.

'Sure! Why not?' said the businessman, unable to pass up a free drink.

They sat on wrought-iron chairs in the merchant's yard and set their beers on an upturned trashcan that served as a table, and together watched the sun sink low behind the distant outline of the city.

'So, do you make a decent living out of all this?' asked the businessman. He was dressed in an expensive suit and had slick hair that gleamed improbably in the evening light.

'Yes, sir. Doin' pretty well for myself,' said the merchant.

The businessman cast his eyes around the yard and looked sceptical.

'Low outlay, high yield,' the merchant continued, eager to present himself as a successful entrepreneur with sound business acumen. 'The world's awash in trash, y'see. Full of crap that nobody wants. Folks even pay *me* to haul it away!

Then I sell it on. I literally make cash outta trash. Not bad, eh?'

'Literally?!' The businessman laughed. 'I think you mean figuratively.'

Behind the city, the setting sun streaked the sky blood-red.

'But that'd be the thing, wouldn't it,' mused the businessman. 'I mean, if you *literally* could turn trash into cash. Then you'd be set for life, buddy!' He chuckled. 'It's a shame you're not in that market.'

The merchant, a little rankled at being called 'buddy' and feeling his pride prickle under the businessman's disdainful gaze, took a hearty swig of his beer and leaned in close.

'Well,' he said, conspiratorially, 'maybe that's where you're wrong, buddy.'

You know, perhaps, how this story goes?

How the vain merchant, so desperate to impress, puffs himself up with nothing but hot air and hyperbole. What preposterous claims he makes.

Impossible!

Outrageous!

Unhinged!

But I'm sure I don't need to tell you how, sometimes, such delicious possibilities, told with great conviction, can become almost believable.

And so it is that the merchant — fool that he is! — offers up the one good and true thing in his life to satisfy the momentary gnawing of his ego. Even though tomorrow, in the cold light of day, he'll weep bitterly and will barely be able to believe he was capable of such stupidity.

'Give my daughter the most stinking trash, and she'll turn it, *literally*, into money. *Actual money*,' said the merchant.

He paused to give the businessman time to absorb his words.

'Give her garbage; she'll give you greenbacks!' He was getting into his stride now. 'She'll spin shit into spondoolix! Yes, indeed! My daughter can make muck into money!'

The businessman was intrigued.

He eyed the merchant's daughter across the scrapyard; she was young and pretty, and if these claims were true, also in possession of an extraordinary talent! He could do much worse, he thought. Much worse. 'You don't say?'

'I do say.'

And that, as they say, was that.

*

In the businessman's penthouse apartment, high in the teetering city, the girl sat surrounded by stinking buckets of food scraps that her new husband had gathered from the streets of the city before the composting truck had had chance to collect them. He'd be back tomorrow, he said, and he expected to see results!

The smell was overpowering; a stench spun of a thousand and one cast-off meals. It was both lush and rancid, ripe and fetid, fresh and fermented. A foul olfactory fabric seemingly woven of fruit and fish and vomit. It swirled around her, wild and awful, and she had to hold her breath so as not to throw up.

Of course, the girl had no idea how she might turn that pile of detritus into dollar bills.

She sat at the window. For safety reasons, the window could be opened only slightly and uselessly at the very top, but she did so anyway — to let a slip of sticky air wend its way inside and to let a little of the stink eke out. She watched the city rumbling far below. Occasionally, helicopters flew by — pursuing criminals or rushing people to hospital. Perhaps, she thought, she might reach out to one — leap aboard and be carried far away. But she knew, of course, that such ideas were quite foolish.

There was a tale she remembered, perhaps it was one her mother had told her long ago, about a girl stranded in a tower whose hair grew so long that a handsome prince climbed it and rescued her.

She knew, however, that she did not have the right kind of hair to inhabit such a tale. Her hair was tightly curled and slow growing, turning in on itself like a dense root. Even if she had waited for many years it would never have grown long and sleek enough to be knotted into an effective ladder. Besides, she did not have years — she had only until the next day, when her husband would return from his business trip, by which time she must have completed her impossible task.

As she sat and wept, certain that she would perish (plunging, perhaps, to her death from such a window, for although she did not know exactly what would happen to her if she could not fulfil her father's insane promise, she knew that it would be terrible) she heard someone whistling outside the apartment door. She went to the front door and looked through the peephole and saw, in the hallway, a man pushing a cart laden with assorted brooms and hoses and tools. A janitor, she assumed.

He was a rumpled man — dressed in brown overalls that resembled a crinkled paper bag, and the skin of his face hung like folds of cloth, although he did not appear to be particularly old. Rather, it seemed to her, somewhat eerily, that he had pulled on someone else's clothes along with their skin, and that neither fit him very well.

The man looked up towards the door of the apartment, and although he could not possibly have seen her there on the other side of the door watching him through the little peephole, he appeared to meet her gaze directly, and to lift his saggy jowls into a seeming-smile.

You know, I'm sure, what happens next.

She opens the door.

He sees the weeping girl. So pretty and so young. Why then, he asks, so sad and hopeless?

So she tells him her unlikely predicament. She points to the stinking pile of trash inside. And incredibly, he is unfazed by this extraordinary tale, and he says that perhaps, if she'd like, he might be able to assist her.

She says she'll pay him whatever she can — anything! Anything at all, if he really can help her.

And she embraces him, this strange and rumpled man, crying tears of relief and gratitude and heady hope.

And she lets him in.

He told her it would take some time, so she put some coffee on.

'Milk?' she said.

'Nope,' he said. 'I take it black and strong, ma'am.'

'Sugar?'

'Yes, ma'am. Three spoonfuls,' he said.

She poured a cup for him, and one for herself, into the little glass mugs that the businessman kept in his immaculate kitchen.

As she carried the coffee through, she saw him unravelling the cord of a shining silver machine that he'd had affixed to his cart — she'd thought at first it was a vacuum, although now as she looked closer, she saw it was much smaller and stranger, and covered in many elaborate dials and knobs. He saw her watching and glanced up at her, his eyes cold and stern, and she flushed with the sudden thought that this man who had offered to help her might intend to do her harm.

'I'll need to be completely alone, ma'am,' he said. 'It's a confidential procedure. I'm sure you understand?'

'Oh,' she said. 'Of course.'

Since the apartment was open-plan, there was nowhere for her to go, so he suggested she wait in the kitchen closet.

She sat, sipping her coffee in the darkness, reflecting on how ridiculous it was to be sitting there amongst the tinned food and cleaning supplies. But then, she thought, the whole situation she found herself in was somewhat ridiculous. She listened to the whirr of the mysterious machine for what seemed like hours. When the whirring finally stopped, she peeked out of the door.

'Are you done?' she asked.

'Yes, ma'am,' he said.

She stepped out and saw, to her astonishment, that the apartment was filled with money — more money than she had ever seen in her life. It was piled high like swept-up leaves, and it completely buried the rug, the coffee table and the couches in the living area. In the faint breeze from the air conditioning unit, the bills rustled.

'Thank you!' she cried. 'You've saved me! However can I thank you?'

'Well,' he said, letting his eyes slide over her. 'What do you have?'

She thought for a moment and patted her pockets. She had no jewellery, no money — although to offer him money would have been absurd in the circumstances. 'I've got an iPhone,' she said.

It hadn't worked anyway since she'd arrived at the penthouse. It seemed unlikely, she thought, but perhaps it was simply too high up for even the cell phone signals to reach.

'What model?' he said. 'Six?'

'Four,' she said, handing it to him.

He frowned and turned the phone over in his hands. 'All right,' he said at last. 'That'll do nicely, ma'am.'

The businessman, returning later in the morning, was delighted with his wife's work.

He drove around the city until dusk, gathering compost buckets from the neighbourhoods who were due to have their bins collected the following day, and returned with even more trash than before, stinking more rankly and piled even higher.

'I'm flying out for an early morning meeting now,' he said as he left. 'I'll be back later tomorrow. Do your magic, honey!'

That evening, the strange man arrived as before.

Again, she waited in the closet with her coffee while he busied himself with the trash. This time though, she was prepared and took her laptop in with her and watched a movie. There was no internet, because the businessman did not have Wi-Fi in his apartment. She wasn't sure why — perhaps he didn't want it, or perhaps he'd disconnected it so she couldn't message for help. Not that it mattered. There was no one she might have contacted anyway, and surely no one would have believed her preposterous story.

When the man had finished, she stepped out of her closet and saw an even greater pile of money than the first. It filled the living room and spilled into the kitchen and buried the bed, covering the floor as high as her knees. She had to wade through it like so much fallen snow.

She started to thank the man, but he interrupted her, 'Well, what have you got for me this time?'

Before she could answer, his eyes settled on the laptop that she was holding folded in her arms against her chest. 'Is that a Mac?'

'Erm, no,' she said.

'Let me see it.'

She handed it to him and he turned it over in his hands. He picked at a small scratch on the back and narrowed his eyes critically.

'OK, ma'am, I'll take it,' he said. 'Same time tomorrow then?'

Of course, the businessman was overjoyed to see the mountain of money when he returned. And, of course, he presented his wife with an even larger, even fouler mountain of garbage that evening. Just once more, he said, and then she could relax. He was so proud of her! What a catch she was! And he kissed her on the cheek, and told her he'd be home around lunchtime the next day.

When the man arrived, she made him coffee and waited in the closet as she had before, listening to the hum of his machine as he worked. The hours rolled by slowly and she regretted the loss of her laptop and wished she had something to occupy her in the dark cupboard.

She fell eventually into a fitful, uncomfortable sleep. And when she woke and opened the door, she saw a pile of money even larger than the previous two. It stuffed the apartment; it blocked the doorways and obscured the windows so that even though the dawn was now breaking outside, the apartment was still black as night. Notes swirled in the air, and a few even drifted out of the tiny crack of the open window.

'Thank you! Thank you so much!' she said.

'All part of the service, ma'am.'

'But you know, don't you, that I have nothing else to give you.'

The man looked her up and down. He was silent for a moment.

'Your first-born child,' he said, just as casually as could be.

He took a final slurp of cold coffee.

She said nothing. This was not what she had expected.

Why, you might well ask, does she agree to such a terrible bargain?

You can imagine, I'm sure, that she has given much thought to the problem of how she might pay the man. Awaiting his arrival, she's watched the sky darken and the city lights flicker on, turning the question over in her mind. And all night, sitting alone in the closet, her thoughts have grown ever darker, because she knows with sickening certainty that there is only one thing a woman in her position might have to offer.

What she feared he would ask for is something both horrifying and immediate, so this proposal when it comes — so bizarre and distant — seems to her almost a relief, a kind of reprieve.

In any case, the girl is not the kind of girl who loves children. She has never imagined herself as a mother, and in truth, she finds babies slightly disgusting. They always smell so ripe and sour, of milk and soiled diapers — a smell, she thinks, that is not unlike the piles of composting food she has recently grown so familiar with.

So it is easy for her to agree to give up something that she does not have now, that she does not even want, and that she cannot imagine ever having.

Which, perhaps, you can appreciate — after all, isn't it easy for any of us to agree to pay an unimaginable price far off in the uncharted future?

'Not straight away,' the man said. 'Too much trouble when they're very small, you see. But after about a year — that's the best time.'

And although the sinister bargain did not seem quite real

to her, she nevertheless began to feel a dank well of dread pooling in her stomach.

'Is it a deal, then?' he said, tapping his foot impatiently.

'I suppose so,' she said.

He grinned. And almost too quickly to see, although she could swear she did see it, he licked his lips.

'Good doing business with you, ma'am,' he said.

And that was that.

*

Time passed, as it has a way of doing. The girl grew used to her new life in her new home. Her husband travelled a great deal for his work, so she was often alone, looking out from her high perch over the glittering city. When he returned, he would shower her with gifts, and they would eat elaborate dinners in dazzling restaurants. She wore the sleek, black dresses he bought for her, and her neck and ears sparkled with diamonds.

In a way, she grew fond of her husband. Or at least, she resigned herself to her life with him. And after all, she reflected, he had never actually been unkind to her, and he gave her such beautiful, precious things.

And so, eventually it happened that she became pregnant.

The girl, or perhaps we should call her a woman now, was surprised to find that pregnancy pleased her. She spent the long, empty days in the penthouse enchanted by her rounding belly, delighted by the little fluttering kicks and hiccups of the baby growing inside her.

And when, finally, he was born, she loved her son beyond all imagining.

It seemed to her that she was made new: everything that had happened to her up until that point — the years of her marriage, and before that, her childhood with her father, and

177

the already-fading memories of her mother — seemed to belong to another time, or to someone else's life. There was only this; only now. Which is why, perhaps, she forgot entirely about her bargain with the strange man and the promise she had made, so long ago, when she had not dreamed she would ever become a mother.

Months passed and she basked in her beautiful boy. His cherubic cheeks! His bowed lips! She adored the smell of him, and spent hours nuzzling the scent of his hair and skin. Even his diapers delighted her, and made her think of sun-drenched farmyards where contented cows munched on hay and made sweet manure.

He was full of such mystery, she thought. When he slept, she would watch him dreaming his secret little dreams, and when he fed, he would hum softly and intently, as if singing some sweet, strange hymn to her breast.

She revelled in the unexpected beauty of it, that she could make milk for him. And she would watch him, wonderingly, when he fed, and he would sometimes reach out to twist her hair, or to grasp her hand and pull on her fingers in turn, like levers, as if he believed he were operating some ineffable machinery that brought him milk.

By turns, he learned to sit up, to shuffle and crawl and pull along the furniture, until one evening, when they were alone (her husband was away, as he often was, on business in Europe), the boy took his first, teetering steps. And, just as her son toddled back to her and fell into her arms, both of them laughing with delight at his new accomplishment, she heard from outside the door a chilling and familiar whistling. And she remembered — how could she ever have forgotten! — the strange, rumpled man and the terrible debt he had come to claim.

She did not offer him coffee this time.

She pleaded with him, threatened him, shouted and railed at him. She begged him to take something else — anything else. Did he want money? Or perhaps, she said, her husband had many connections — they could arrange to find the man a position of great power in the city, if he wanted that? Even herself. Yes, he could take her, she said. If only he would spare her child.

But at all this he only laughed and said, 'No, no, no! A deal's a deal!'

She wept and implored, and eventually the man grew serious.

He pulled a slip of paper from his chest pocket. He held it up and turned it over so that she could see it was blank. And, once more, he presented her with a most curious proposal.

'How about this?' he said. 'A word — I'll write a word of my choosing on this piece of paper. Any word at all. And if you can guess it correctly, you can keep the child.'

It was the only hope she had, so she agreed.

At his suggestion, she waited in the closet with the baby while he wrote the word on the paper. Then, he said, she should sign the back of it so that she could see afterwards that it was the very same piece of paper and that he had not tricked her. He wanted to be fair, he said, keep everything above board.

'I'll come three times — give you three chances, ma'am. But I'm betting you won't guess it.'

All the first day, she paced the apartment racking her brains for the mysterious word.

A magical word, she thought at last. It must be a magical word!

She began to remember stories she had heard long ago, where magical words opened doors. And weren't there particular words that invoked the devil? Or pleased the Lord? And she half-remembered, she was sure of it, tales of words that were the true names of things and people — where if you spoke them aloud you would have absolute power over the bearer of the name.

But it was impossible to conjure such words — where to begin?

She wrote down all the magical words she could think of: *Abracadabra! Alakazam! OpenSesame!* — and every nonsensical, childish incantation — *Jinx! Ollyollyoxenfree! Supercalifragilisticexpialidocious!* — and every prayer, every invocation, every plea to every god she knew — *Hallelujah! OmShanti! KrishnaKrishnaHareHare!* — and when she had exhausted herself and could think of no more, she sat and wept.

When the man arrived that evening, she read the list to him.

But each time, he shook his head and chuckled. 'Nope!' he cried. 'That ain't the word!'

'That's all I have,' she said, eventually.

'I'll be back tomorrow,' he said. 'Maybe you'll have better luck then, ma'am. But I doubt it!'

The next day, she tried a different tack. Perhaps, she thought, the word was not magical. Perhaps it was something quite obvious and ordinary. Perhaps when he'd chosen the word, he had simply looked around and selected something in plain view. Even something right in front of her now? She surveyed the apartment, noting down every item that might have caught his eye — *coffee, sugar, mug, vacuum, couch, closet, window, trashcan, door* — and prayed that she might uncover the word.

But, alas, when she read her list to him that evening, once again he cackled at each suggestion and cried, 'Nope! That ain't the word!'

And she spent the night in sleepless despair, for she had only one more chance remaining.

As the third day dawned, she tried to enjoy what might be her last hours with her boy. She watched him toddling delicately about the apartment with his newfound steps. She savoured the weight of him stretched across her when he nursed (for although he was no longer a tiny infant he still reached for her chest and nuzzled her when he needed comfort, and would not fall asleep without it).

Today, however, when his nap-time came and he made the familiar grumble and reached for her shirt and she picked him up, he did something he had not done before: he indicated her breast and, quite clearly, spoke a word.

She looked at him and said the word herself, questioningly, and he said it once more. Three times she repeated the word, and three times he pointed, quite clearly, and said it back to her.

Yes, she thought, this was his first word!

She laughed. What an ordinary alchemy it was — her child making language to speak about his little world. And how surprising, she thought, that he had taken that sweet thing that they had shared wordlessly all this time and given it a name. She picked him up and kissed his hair, and held him long and tight, and wished with all her heart that she would not lose her precious child.

The evening came, and with it the man.

He swung open the apartment door, although she could swear she had locked it tight, and stood in the doorway, tapping his foot and grinning.

'Please!' she said. 'Please don't—'

'*Please?*' he interrupted. 'Oh no, ma'am. That ain't the word!'

'No!' she cried, 'No! I didn't mean—'

'Is that your next guess? *No?* Ha! Nope, that ain't the word either!' He cackled with glee. 'Try again!'

What is she to do?

She has no words left, nothing to give.

And yet her boy — so new and so small, clings to her like a vine, and she must do anything she can to save him. He whines and pulls at her shirt, because he is frightened to see his mother cry and wants to be secure again, wants the sweet comfort of her.

And when she finally offers up a word, it is not because she thinks it is the word she needs — how can it be? Impossible! Outrageous! — but because it is the only one she can find.

She speaks it aloud, that first real word that her child made.

That word that did not even exist until today.

At hearing the word, the man's face contorted hideously.

'What?!' he screeched. 'How could you have known?! You cheated! You saw! You spied on me! Damn you to hell!'

He ripped the paper from his pocket and threw it to the floor and stamped on it.

And then, all the while emitting a gruesome shriek, he ran across the apartment to the window and leapt out. She was not sure how exactly, for it happened so quickly and was so surprising, and she had not believed that anyone could possibly fit through the little crack of the window that let in only a trickle of sticky air.

She followed, carrying her baby on her hip, to look out of the window to see if it were true. And sure enough, there he was, sailing high above the darkening city — not falling, but somehow soaring — and was he, she thought, even riding on that little machine of his? Yes! She could see the silver glinting in the light cast by the other penthouses as he flew past them. And then he was almost too high for her to see — just a speck in the dusky sky, now catching the light with a sudden flash, now melting into the evening.

And then he was gone entirely.

She stood and watched at the window as night fell and the moon rose and the city glittered alive, and she felt suddenly, inexpressibly tired — no wonder, surely, after everything that had happened.

She carried her boy to the bed and they lay down side by side in the darkness. She fed him until they both drifted into a milky sleep, as they had done many times before. And as so many mothers and their little ones had done long before our tale began, and surely will do long after it's over.

Notes on Stories

About 'Rumpelstitskin'

The settings and events of fairy tales might be fantastical, but the emotional dynamics are rooted in a solid and recognisable reality. It always struck me that although the miller in Rumpelstiltskin loves his daughter, he doesn't love her unconditionally. In my telling of this traditional tale, the miller's daughter chooses to give away a vital part of herself — her creativity — in order to win her father's approval.

When we compromise ourselves like this to please others, there are bound to be consequences.

This is a story about creativity: what it is and where it comes from. How we can choose to nurture and honour it, or else neglect or betray it. About how easily inspiration comes sometimes, and how easily it can be squandered.

I didn't realise what this story was about — I mean, about for me personally — until long after it was finished. But looking back I realised I'd made a series of decisions where I'd sacrificed my creativity on the altar of being 'clever', or perhaps simply squandered it because it felt too difficult and too terrifying to tell the stories I was interested in telling. At the time, I was rethinking some of those decisions, and committing to give more of my time and energy to writing. The story came to me complete, almost in a flash, and I wrote it very quickly, not understanding it at all.

Ridiculous, I know, but sometimes these things happen that way.

I also realise that in this story I've explicitly linked creativity with having children, a theme that comes up time and time again in my writing.

I chose to write this story in a traditional manner, using the structure, voice, and some of the language of traditional fairy tales. Having said that, there is more emotional shading than would be the case in say, a Grimm's tale, and greater ambiguity, particularly in the ending, which is possibly more suited to the expectations of modern audiences.

REBECCA ANN SMITH

About 'Hansel's Trouble'

What I've always loved about fairytales is the symmetry, the patterns — so neat, and straightforward. The language is bold, blunt and repetitious. Plots are simple but horrific: 'happily ever after' silences the terror of the tale just told.

When I wrote 'Hansel's Trouble', our first child, Sophie, was about eight months old. Certain fairy tale horrors seemed more horrific than they had previously: absent parents; babies bargained away; children unloved, unwanted, alone.

We didn't know much about babies when Sophie was born, but we read a lot of books and 'attachment' came up a lot. Breastfeeding came easily, and when she wasn't feeding we held her close, co-sleeping at night and carrying her in a sling during the day. We did whatever we could to keep her calm, close and content. When she cried, every nerve in my body told me to make it all right again. Immediately. She's almost three years old now, and both she and Ted, her twenty-month-old brother, are still breastfeeding, co-sleeping and are sometimes slung. Hopefully, they are securely attached, and will be fortunate enough to remain so.

I reread Grimms' 'Hansel and Grethel'. In the first version, the children's mother was never mentioned and had presumably suffered some gruesome fate during the children's early years, before their father remarried. A subsequent version inferred that the children still lived with both birth parents when they were abandoned once, and then again. I'm not sure which version is worse. But on their eventual return to the family abode, laden with the wealth of the cooked witch, the mother/stepmother has died, and the children and their father — this father who, despite misgivings, twice abandoned them in the depths of the forest, fully aware that they would likely be eaten by wild animals — the children and *this* father "lived together happily". Really? I just wasn't convinced. So I wrote 'Hansel's Trouble', while my baby fed and slept on my lap.

LINDSEY WATKINS

About 'Grimm Reality'

My aim is to add magic to a world which is skewed to the rational. The growing number of adults reading, enjoying and blogging about children's books is testament to the quality of writing and the longing for magic.

C. S. Lewis makes the point that there are two types of longing: one is an askesis, a spiritual exercise; the other is a disease. Fairy tales address the former, materially aspirational novels, the latter. Grimm Reality brings them together.

I live in an area where people routinely see nature spirits and make small talk with angels. The consensual aspect of group reality in Glastonbury allows for fairies and angels. A fairy tourist would not be asked for proof of ID. The door policy would be stricter in a city, where urban realism dominates the group mind. Then a fairy sighting would be an epiphany. That was the starting point of my story.

Lewis also argued that morals should not be imposed on a story. Rather they should rise naturally from the roots a writer has struck during the course of her life. I didn't set out to illustrate a moral. What surfaced was the contrast between a set of morals gleaned from fairy tales and the moral shiftiness learned from fashion and celebrity magazines. Other preoccupations remained beneath the surface. What is imagination? In what sense do objects of imagination exist? Are there infinite individual realities? Where do we fix our own borders between reality and imagination? Are we real or imagined and who might be imagining us?

ANA SALOTE

About 'Bear, Hare and Ptarmigan'

My sister Tricia was seven years older than me. She showed me the way in most things as confidante, mentor and counsellor. Tricia saved my skin on many occasions and never mentioned the saving ever again. Even if she had not been my sister, I would have tried to win her as a friend.

She was supersmart and superstylish. When I was fifteen she let me borrow her clothes and told me I should read *Catcher in the Rye*. When I was in my twenties she gave me a copy of Angela Carter's thrillingly dark fairy tales, *The Bloody Chamber*.

Tricia died of cancer almost four years ago. She gave me the last birthday presents she would ever give me six weeks before she died (although none of us, not even she, knew it would be so soon). My three gifts were wrapped in blue tissue; a bottle of Marc Jacobs scent 'Rain' — blue liquid in a square bottle — an oval turquoise brooch and a book with a blue cover. The book was called *Burning Your Boats*, the collected stories of Angela Carter.

A year ago I was in the second term of a short story course at Warwick University and its theme was 'The Fairy Tale'. We looked at the work of writers such as Carter and Ludmilla Petrushevskaya and the assignment for the term was to produce a short story containing fantastical elements. I'd been struck by a Margaret Atwood quote, "All writing of the narrative kind, and perhaps all writing, is motivated, deep down, by a fear of and a fascination with mortality — by a desire to make the risky trip to the Underworld, and to bring something or someone back from the dead." I knew the story I had to write.

I don't believe in an afterlife but I do believe that an intense focus of concentration can retrieve the essence of a person in memory to the extent that a kind of intervention is made possible. This was certainly my experience as I wrote my story. Whole paragraphs were abandoned then rewritten as Tricia intervened. I spent most of the time crying. For me, it was catharsis.

Tricia would say that a happy ending is potentially the weakest part of any story but I know she would be proud and pleased by the happy ending I have created for myself. I can just hear her...

JULIE PEMBERTON

About the 'Jungle Goddess'

I think the story 'Jungle Goddess' had been brewing inside me for a long time before I actually wrote it down on paper.

Many years ago when I lived in India I had read a newspaper article describing how a girl in some remote village had been married off first to a tree and then to a man. An astrologer had apparently told them her first husband was fated to die soon after the wedding! The story stayed with me often attracting to itself other such myths and folklore until I began to wonder what would happen if the stakes were higher.

Many cultures have this archetypal fairy tale of an ogre who lives outside the village gates and threatens to devour all unless he is fed and kept happy. So, often the solution is to send one person at a time until it is the turn of the hero or heroine, who then ends up killing the ogre and freeing the village.

The 'Jungle Goddess' is a mix of the two stories but underlying it was my desire to explore how a society views women. A woman is often defined by the role she plays — a daughter, sister, wife, mother and not by who she really is. Imagine then if the role of a saviour is thrust upon her, or worse, that of a goddess! She would be robbed of her very right to be human and thus lose her right to any empathy and compassion.

Oh, the irony then, when this is done so that other women may become mothers with the blessings of the goddess.

ANURADHA GUPTA

About 'Mirror, Mirror'

I have long been interested in the retelling of myths and fairy tales, stories that are so ingrained in our society that they become part of us, expected norms and teachings on how to behave and view ourselves, especially as women. To subvert these stories is to subvert how we think about ourselves, our relationships, and our lives. One writer who thoroughly explored the twists and turns of fairy tales and how they can be reinterpreted was Angela Carter. Through post-modernism, magical realism, and feminism, she examined and reimagined women's places within these tales.

I completed an MA in Creative and Critical Writing, with a thesis on the imagery of the mirror in Angela Carter's short fiction. This led me to my own retelling of the 'Snow White' story, which was to become my piece 'Mirror, Mirror'. This version shows how women's identity is often linked to image, and how that image is often that of the other; and in this case, represented by the magic mirror, who leads the princess' stepmother to focus on being the fairest of them all. This stepmother is as much a victim as Snow White. A victim of her society and of her circumstances. Once this is realised, there is the potential to change the story and both the princess and her stepmother regain their own power, independence, and freedom.

LAURA KAYNE

About 'Seal Woman'

It's funny that when you look back at how and when things happen in your life, the memories rarely feel linear. At the time just before I retold this Seal Woman story I felt alienated from the world of myth and folk tales, and frustrated by my disconnection. It felt like a lack of roots. Growing up in the South of England, and living in a place where the land is systematically being concreted over, it's sometimes hard to make contact with the stories that belong to the place; hard to walk the Songlines. When meeting storytellers from Wales, Ireland and Scotland it's struck me how strongly they belong to their land, their stories and mythological heritage, and I've felt wistful. As if something was missing.

But at the same time, my life has always been rich with novels with mythic undercurrent like Catherine Fisher's *Corbenic*; Kevin Crossley Holland's *Arthur* trilogy; Juliet Marillier's *Sevenwaters* series. These stories weave myth, folk tale and original story in such a way that each reveals something surprising in the other in endless equilibrium. It was my ambition to one day achieve some semblance of this in my own writing.

And somewhere in the midst of this, *Women Who Run With the Wolves*, in all its wild earthiness, arrived. This book, along with the novels, gave folk tales back to me. Inspired by Clarissa Pinkola Esté's retelling of the Seal Woman story, and moved by the tale's ancient themes of ecstatic being, of love and loss and soul hunger, I wrote my own version but from the seal woman's point of view. Previously, I'd only ever seen this story told from the perspective of the fisherman. How strange! And so here was my point of ignition; and for the first time I felt I belonged to a story. I didn't need a particular place. I was the place.

In attempting to bring this story alive, I also came alive within it. I felt that wonderful ultra-dimensional mystery, that archetypal resonance that only the old tales bring. I am so thankful for this. And so happy to be in this lovely anthology that celebrates that deep, wild magic.

RACHEL RIVETT

About 'Icarus'

It's a truism, I think, that writers take their material from life: true enough perhaps, but experience is likely to be heavily shaped by the requirements of the writing, through which it becomes something else. 'Icarus' was inspired by a (true) story of Allied prisoners of war held in the castle at Colditz in Germany in the early 1940s. The castle is an imposing edifice perched atop an outcrop above the town, and the Germans considered it escape-proof. They were proved wrong on several occasions, and even on reading the first-hand accounts of these times, it's hard to avoid the somewhat adventuresome tone of their narratives. The most spectacular of these escapes never took place, though it was planned and executed to near-completion, only being rendered obsolete at the last minute by the eventual liberation of Colditz. Several prisoners did indeed construct a glider from bed parts behind a fake wall in the attic, with the intention of launching it from the roof, across the river, and into the fields away from the town, from where the two occupants could make a run for it. There are many more stories of tunnels and disguises, and they are all extraordinary, but the glider stuck in my mind as an image of freedom over all the rest — flight, after all, being potently symbolic in this way.

I was very conscious while writing this piece of avoiding romanticising warfare and imprisonment, but I adpoted some of the stylisations of fairy tales and myths — particularly the repetitive structure and the perhaps rather obvious title — to try to imbue my version of the story with something less specific to the horrors of that war, and more resonant with the general human desire to be free.

I leave the conclusion to the reader.

NATHAN RAMSDEN

About 'Lilasette'

I have loved fairy tales from my early childhood — I borrowed Andrew Lang's *Red, Yellow, Lilac, Grey*, and other colourful *Fairy Books* from the Brooklyn Public Library over and over again, and lost myself in the stories of princesses, witches, enchanted animals, and forests that held secrets and magic.

So it was no accident, I suppose, that my career path led eventually to editing and then writing children's books — and that many of the books I wrote were adaptations and retellings of the classic fairy tales I had loved as a child. Reading — and retelling — these stories again and again drew me into them even more, and I became increasingly interested in exploring why they have such enduring power.

The stories that have always spoken to me most are the ones that focussed on difficult mother-daughter relationships, probably because of the complex and difficult relationship I had with my own mother. When, in my late 50s, I did an MA in Folklore and Cultural Tradition at the University of Sheffield, I focussed my research on fairy tales, and in particular the stepmother figure in 'Snow White'. (Interestingly, in the Grimms' original version of 'Snow White', the wicked queen was Snow White's mother, not her stepmother.) My studies reinforced for me the great psychological power of fairy tales. The work I did for my degree began to seep into the retellings and adaptations I was commissioned to write professionally and led, inevitably, to my writing fairy tales of my own.

'Lilasette' explores the mother-daughter relationship in a way that is very personal to me. Lilacs are my favourite flower, and my mother loved them too — smelling lilacs with my mother when I was very, very small is a happy memory for me, and it stands out from the many painful memories I have of her as I grew up. That was the starting point for the story;

the name, 'Lilasette' just came to me as I wrote it.

Many thanks to Teika Bellamy for encouraging me to finish the story. I started it not long after I finished my MA, then put it aside. It was a chance meeting with Teika at the Five Leaves bookshop in Nottingham, and learning about Mother's Milk Books and this anthology, that prompted me to finish the tale. I'm so glad I did — it has been a powerful and in many ways a healing experience.

RONNE RANDALL

About 'The Worm'

I grew up in Northumberland so the story of the 'Lambton Worm' is one I was very familiar with. The most famous version of the story is in the form of a dialect poem written in 1867 by C. M. Leumane. The North Eastern dialect is very specific and very strong so is often inaccessible to people who are not from the originating area. I was always fascinated by the story and when I started to think of ideas for *The Forgotten and the Fantastical 2* it was one of the first stories that came to mind. At first I had planned a simpler retelling, purely for the purpose of translating the dialect poem into a more accessible form. I should have known from the start that my propensity for writing stories with ambiguous or even downright unhappy endings would take this particular retelling down a completely different path. Sometimes the story you are telling knows what it wants to be before you even know yourself.

In the original story the worm is the most unflinchingly one-dimensional representation of a dragon, monstrous, vicious, a plague on the Lambton estate. As I was writing my story the worm became something different altogether. The further through the writing process I got the more uncomfortable I was with the idea of the worm as a one-dimensional character. It was quite early on that the idea that the young lord would actually be fond of this monster, perhaps even love it, and then still have to kill it came to me.

The original story ends with the young lord being forced to choose between killing his father or condemning nine generations of Lambtons to violent deaths far from their own deaths. The Lambtons were a real family and the curse did appear to hold true for at least three generations. This is possibly why the legend remained so popular for so long. I chose to finish my story immediately after the moral and emotional ambiguity of killing the worm as I felt that continuing after this would result in the loss of some of the power of the young lord's emotional response to the death.

SARAH HINDMARSH

About 'Paths of Desire'

Maybe being named Fionnula, from the Irish 'The Children of Lir', gave me an early love of fairy tales and legends. As a child my companion bedside reading was a very old fairy tale book, crammed with tales from Grimm to Perrault with dark Rackman illustrations. Princesses and babes were constantly being risked and rescued. Thankfully, I later found Angela Carter's wonderful rewriting. Ursula Le Guin's work was also important in re-imagining the myths.

I find the Selkies especially fascinating. They are a good metaphor perhaps for many women who feel a lack of control, who are trapped, wanting to leave but unable to. The starting point to my story, the image of the women whose mouths were stitched tightly closed, came in a dream!

I also wanted to examine the pressure that trying to conceive can put on a couple, as well as commenting on the role of women once they are past childbearing age. One thing I was determined to do was to give the central character the power of action. I also wanted to show the pressure on men to carry on the family line. It was important to avoid simply blaming the man, who is struggling with his own problems.

My characters, like so many of us, solve their problems by taking risks, by picking up and starting again. Crucially they work together, supporting and encouraging each other.

FINOLA SCOTT

About 'How Women Came to Love Mirrors'

When I wrote 'How Women Came to Love Mirrors' twenty years ago I intended only to write a very simple story. The driving force behind it was my passion for a 'magical' world where emotional being can manifest as a physical reality. The character, Anna, starts to intermittently disappear as her inner life is literally revealed. She has no control of what is happening to her, but to survive she must find a kind of solution.

Anna is, I suppose, 'me' and my interpretation of what happens everywhere to women. In the story this is exaggerated from the beginning in that her very name is taken from her. But women everywhere live in partial invisibility, still, and despite it being a familiar feminist position. What I wish to uncover most in this story is how we bear this in our souls. By this I mean that if we turned outward what we feel inward, what would be seen? My answer is the confusing loss of materiality that Anna experiences; the embodied not-knowing or believing who we are; the vulnerability we feel. Searching for our power and voice is a great journey for women, and now, twenty years after writing this story, I think I would have given Anna other solutions. I acknowledge as I reread it that I offered her only a partial remedy; and one that becomes controlled by the male merchant in the story to boot. So rather than having the wisdom to liberate Anna I did what most women do: found a compromise that fits, more or less, the world we live in.

HANNAH MALHOTRA

About 'Fox Fires'

'Fox Fires' was born out of two of my great loves — foxes and the Northern Lights. Unfortunately, living as I do in Manchester, U.K., I don't get to see much of either, so I decided to write about them instead!

I've always found the Aurora to be truly magical and steeped in a rich tradition of mythology. 'Fox Fires' loosely weaves a couple of those strands together into one tale, while also exploring themes of grief, loss and loneliness and how a simple act of kindness can sometimes make all the difference.

I wanted to create a feeling of tradition with this story. I deliberately kept the writing short and the characters nameless as I wanted to evoke a sense of distance across time and for the piece to read like an origin myth in its own right, a sliver of folklore passed down from generation to generation.

I hope you enjoy reading it as much as I enjoyed writing it.

JANE WRIGHT

About 'Solstice'

In a legend of both heroic and dastardly men, Maid Marian was the one female role model that my twelve-year-old self had to cling to. If Marian stays at home and accepts her pre-destined path then there is no woman in Sherwood Forest. If she wants a life of her own, with her lover, then she must go to him.

My favourite Marian is Robin McKinley's in the *Outlaws of Sherwood*. This Marian not only survives outdoors, but in her role as lady of the manor shows a courage and a political astuteness that puts Robin to shame. She is a better archer than Robin and, in disguise, wins the silver arrow in his place. Although this competition is clearly a trap, only Marian understands the need for Robin to be there, and the importance of his fledgling legend to the morale of the Nottingham peasants.

Disney's Maid Marian is also a favourite. Marian the vixen may not be the most active of heroines, but she is true, compassionate and brave.

For me, Marian represents the best of both the traditional sides of a female lead. She is not afraid to embrace her femininity with strength and truth. On the flip side, Marian has also mastered the art of cross-dressing. She can make it in a man's world on her own terms. In either case Marian knows what she wants and is not afraid to follow her own heart. My twelve-year-old self could not have asked for a better life lesson.

DEBORAH OSBORNE

About 'Rêve/Revival'

This story was inspired by two things. The first was an old made-for-TV film of Margot Fonteyn in the ballet of 'Sleeping Beauty'. It is a very magical old film, in black and white, well worth watching. For those not familiar with the ballet version of 'Sleeping Beauty', it contains a whole host of fairies, animals and birds, who come to dance at the palace after Princess Aurora has been restored. This led me to think more deeply about the fairies and the forest, and to imagine a broken relationship with humans that could eventually be restored. I wanted to give the ballet's "evil fairy", Carabosse, a more substantial reason to punish the human rulers than mere spite at an overlooked party invitation. Humans' relationship with nature, particularly at the time of the Industrial Revolution, seemed a good place to start.

The second influence was a book called *Vanished Kingdoms: The History of Half-Forgotten Europe* by Norman Davies. It's quite a heavy-going book of political history, and not always very optimistic about Europe's future, but it does provide a fascinating insight into the way the map changes over many centuries, as countries are annexed or abandoned by more powerful countries, fragment, or gain independence. I was reminded just how much the political map can change over just one century. If you slept for a hundred years — say between 1815 and 1915 — you would wake up in a very different world, and possibly in a different country, from the one you fell asleep in.

The major anniversaries of both Waterloo and the First World War reminded me how drastically both those eras of conflict changed Europe's political landscape. Small states were inevitably the biggest losers, when caught between the clashes of empires. At the end of hostilities in 1815, and even more so in 1918, many states simply ceased to exist, absorbed into Russia/the USSR, France, Germany, Yugoslavia etc. For my tale, I wanted to imagine a small, independent state, struggling to hold its own against more powerful nations. What would happen if that state disappeared from the map, not just in political terms, but more literally? If it became a place where the human and the fey intermingled to form a new and different society, putting their old enmity aside? What if it became a place of refuge from the future collapse of nations? That is the outcome I wanted to explore in 'Rêve/Revival'.

ELIZABETH HOPKINSON

About Little Lost Soul

I'm not entirely sure where 'Little Lost Soul' sprang from, but I can at least try to explain what was swirling round my head — and my environment — when the story began to form. Sometime last year I saw a call for submissions for short stories on the theme of 'Monsters'. This got me thinking about all sorts of 'monstrous' topics and myths, and I went on to write several short stories on this theme. I also decided it was high-time that I wrote some science-fiction (since my background is in science) so on the recommendation of my husband, a sci-fi buff, I began to read the stories of Isaac Asimov. 'Little Lost Robot' was the first story of Asimov's that I read, and so a flavour of this found its way into my story. Being half-Russian and half-Latvian I decided that it was time that one of my stories was set in a place that would be recognizably Soviet-like in nature. My art area, which I share with my children, is covered in pens, paper and paint as well as various inspirational objects. My Russian dolls – *matryoshki* – take pride of place in the art area and watch over me as I draw, and so a little of them seeped into the story too. And lastly... when my children were watching *Newsround* on CBBC I caught a snippet about the latest advances in robotics and I had to wonder at how scarily close we were to walking, talking and thinking robots... It got me asking the questions that all writers need to ask themselves: *What if?* and *Why?*

Many of my stories focus on issues of female psychology and empowerment, and 'Little Lost Soul' is no different. But the real question here is that hoary old chestnut, *What does it mean to be human?*

A while after I finished writing the story I remembered the poem, 'The Forest of Miracles' by one of my favourite poets, Angela Topping. Her phrase 'antique silence' had lodged itself in my mind and I realized that Angela had perfectly described the poem that my heroine — or should that be anti-heroine? — had escaped into. I was so pleased that Angela gave me permission to use it.

MARIJA SMITS

About 'Trash Into Cash'

Rumpelstiltskin has always been my favourite fairy tale. I love how it piles peril upon peril — the heroine is forced into marriage by her own father, then threatened with death if she can't spin straw into gold, before being offered apparent salvation by a strange man who, in return for his assistance, demands her first-born child. Her only chance for escape lies in the seemingly impossible task of discovering his name. It's both nightmarish and beautiful — the impossible tasks like something from a bad dream; the idea that speaking a name aloud might break a spell. And like many fairy tales, it takes our primal, unspeakable terrors — that our loved ones might betray us; that our loved ones might be stolen from us — and in playing them out, seems to make those fears almost bearable.

Having children has given me a chance to rediscover fairy tales, noticing things that I'd forgotten or never knew — for example, when reading to my son I was delighted to find a version of this story that ends with Rumpelstiltskin hopping astride a wooden spoon and flying out of the window! And, of course, the queen's awful bargain with Rumpelstiltskin horrifies me now in a way that it didn't before I'd had children of my own.

Becoming a mother has also had a huge impact on what I want to write about. For instance, I've breastfed both my children into toddlerhood and have found it endlessly fascinating and transformative.

Although our society's attitudes towards breastfeeding are rapidly changing, there are still many taboos about it. It's accepted that small babies need to breastfeed, yet breastfeeding an older baby or child is often viewed as unnecessary, indulgent or even abnormal. However, sustained breastfeeding (beyond the first few months, until one or two years of age or beyond) is a quite ordinary experience for mothers and children in much of the world today, and has been throughout history. This issue is something that I only touch on in my story, but I'd like to think it offers a kind of counterpoint to that claim you often hear: 'When a child is old enough to talk about it, it's definitely time to wean!' Instead, I'm interested in how there's magic and enchantment in the breastfeeding relationship, and how it doesn't always exist for a child purely within the silent blur of pre-consciousness — how sometimes mothers and children might find words to talk about something that so many mothers and children have experienced.

BECKY TIPPER

Index
of Writers with Biographies

Anuradha Gupta (p. 53)

Anuradha Gupta was born in Mumbai, India and has spent the last twenty years travelling to foreign lands and writing about them, at times, even, setting up homes there, which was fantastic as she loves people and places. She now lives in London which has become her much loved home away from home. In 2013 she published a collection of her poems and art called *New Moon Rising*. It continues to gather some wonderful reviews.

She is fascinated by ancient cultures, their myths and legends. She explores her own ancient heritage and culture in her blog: www.allabouthinduism.info

The story 'Jungle Goddess' is her first attempt at fiction.

Sarah Hindmarsh (p. 103)

Sarah Hindmarsh is the author of the Animal Adventures series for children and the 1001 writing prompts series. She has also had poems and stories published by several journals and magazines. Her first children's book 'The Mouse Who Howled at the Moon' was shortlisted for the SpaSpa independent book awards and various works have been nominated for the 2016 SWAN awards. Most of her best ideas come to her while she is walking her miniature poodle, Kohla. Sarah is passionate about encouraging children (and everybody else) to read for pleasure and blogs about issues surrounding children's literacy at: creatingwithkohla.com.

Elizabeth Hopkinson (p. 147)

Elizabeth Hopkinson is a fantasy writer from Bradford, West Yorkshire, UK — home of the Brontë sisters and the Cottingley Fairies. She loves fairy tale and history, especially the 18th century, and is currently writing a trilogy set in a fantasy version of baroque Italy. Her short fiction has appeared in many publications, and her historical fantasy novel, *Silver Hands*, is available from all good book outlets.

Laura Kayne (p. 61)

Laura Kayne lives in Sussex, where she enjoys being by the sea as well as the literary heritage of the area. She has an MA in Creative and Critical Writing and a number of poems, short stories, and reviews published both in print and on-line. These include *Aesthetica* and *The New Writer* magazines, and the Pygmy Giant website. She has had short stories published digitally with Ether Books, and on the Café Lit website. She is currently working on a first pamphlet, which is likely to be science and astronomy themed, being keen to explore links between science and the arts.

Hannah Malhotra (p. 121)

Hannah grew up in a house full of books, reading all the time and dreaming of being a writer. When she was young she fell in love with magical realist writing by Márquez and others, and also loved fairy tales from all over the world. She wrote and published non-fiction in her twenties and kept her fiction hidden in a secret drawer until recently. She is a mother of two who runs a yoga studio in Nottingham and is writing again. Her full name, acknowledging her father, mother and grandmothers, is Hannah Fries Buick Oliver Hickling — and if you have read her story you will see that this is important. Contact her at: hannahmalhotra@gmail.com

Deborah Osborne (p. 139)

Deborah Osborne is an East Saxon currently residing in Kent. She lives on coffee, kisses and cake. One day she will finish revising her first book. In the meantime Deborah writes her own reality at: deborahellenosborne.wordpress.com.

Julie Pemberton (p. 47)

Julie Pemberton lives in the leafy Warwickshire town of Kenilworth with her husband, Graham. She is a former primary school teacher with a Master's degree in children's literature from the University of Warwick. It was whilst working towards this degree that Julie first read Bruno Bettelheim's *The Uses of Enchantment: The Meaning and Importance of Fairy Tales*. Himself a concentration camp survivor who went on to become an eminent psychoanalyst, Bettelheim writes of the power of fairy stories to heal and empower the severely traumatised and disturbed children he treated. This is Julie's first published work and she is delighted that it should be a fairy tale.

NJ Ramsden (p. 83)

Nathan 'NJ' Ramsden writes mostly short fiction, though he keeps meaning to get round to writing that epic novel. Influences include Donald Barthelme, H. P. Lovecraft, J. L. Borges, Angela Carter, classical mythology, and folklore.

He has written two novels (*Nothing's Oblong* and *Scissors/Paper/Stone*) and a screenplay ('Tell Me Lies About Love', based on his short work 'Love Story'), and has had short stories publihsed in print and online. He taught Creative Writing for several years. In his spare time he enjoys baking, translating medieval literature, and makes music with synthesizers and a beaten-up old jazz bass. He can be found online via his irregular blog: njramsden.wordpress.com

Ronne Randall (p. 93)

Ronne Randall was born in New York and has lived in the U.K. since 1985. She has worked in publishing since the late 1960s, and for the last 35 years has written, edited, and Americanized scores of mass-market children's books. She studied English Literature at Brooklyn College many, many decades ago; more recently, her lifelong interest in traditional tales and ballads led her to do an MA in Folklore and Cultural Tradition at the University of Sheffield. Ronne, who is currently working on a memoir of her childhood in Brooklyn, lives with her husband Norman in Nottinghamshire; their grown-up son, Daniel, lives in London.

Rachel Rivett (p. 77)

Author of three picture books, and shortlisted for SCBWI's Undiscovered Voices 2014 with her YA mythic fantasy, *Traitor Girl*, Rachel Rivett has an MA in Writing for Children from Winchester University. She is an aspiring Young Adult author with a love of mythic and dystopian novels; although, as someone famously pointed out, dystopian novels are ever harder to write these days as governments steal all the best ideas for policy making. She and her husband home-educate their four children, (the eldest of whom is now at college), believing the best learning happens when people follow their hearts.

Ana Salote (p. 39)

Ana Salote lives in Somerset. She has recently completed a MG/crossover fantasy trilogy. Book 1, *Oy Yew*, was published by Mother's Milk Books in 2015. Book 2 is due for release in 2016. Her stories have appeared in *Mslexia* and *Midland Exposure*. When she is not writing she roams the wilds and runs a small retail business. Her interests include the environment and alternative societies. She is inspired by all things 'counter, original, spare, strange'.

Finola Scott (p. 111)
Writing since taking early retirement, Glaswegian Finola Scott belongs to several groups, both online and physical. She finds the support of others vital as writing can be a lonely pursuit. Her stories and poems have been placed in and won national competitions and are widely published. This year she was selected as one of the poets to be mentored on the Clydebuilt Scheme. This year, the mentor is the Scottish Makar, Liz Lochhead. Performing is important to Finola as she likes to feel her words in her mouth and ears. She is proud to be a slam-winning Granny!

Rebecca Ann Smith (p. 11)
Rebecca Ann Smith writes novels for adults, teenagers and children. Her first published novel, *Baby X* is a psychological thriller about medical ethics and motherhood set against the backdrop of advances in fertility treatment. *Baby X* will be published by Mother's Milk Books in summer 2016.

Rebecca is interested in creativity, feminism and social justice, and blogs about these topics and others at: rebeccaannsmith.co.uk.

She lives in West Sussex with her husband and two sons.

Marija Smits (p. 155)
Marija Smits is a mother-of-two, a writer and artist whose work has featured in a variety of publications. Her work is rather eclectic and she loves semi-colons, as well as plenty of cream in her coffee. She is a member of the Nottingham Writers' Studio. For more on some of her favourite topics, such as high sensitivity, please visit: marijasmits.wordpress.com

Becky Tipper (p. 165)

Becky Tipper writes short fiction and non-fiction, often inspired by her experiences as a mother. Her writing has appeared in several anthologies and journals, including *Literary Mama*, *Mom Egg Review* and the Bridport Prize anthology, and her prose was 'commended' in the 2014 Mother's Milk Books Writing Prize. Her latest short story (which also explores pregnancy and parenthood) will be published in *Prole* magazine (April 2016). She is British but now lives in the US with her husband, her son (aged 7) and her daughter (aged 2).

Lindsey Watkins (p. 31)

Lindsey Watkins lives in West Yorkshire with her wife and two young children. She spends large portions of each day tandem breastfeeding two toddlers whilst reading a stack of picture books. In between requests for 'milky', Lindsey works as a high-school English teacher and also tries to fit in a bit of reading, writing and rock-climbing where she can.

Jane Wright (p. 131)

Jane Wright is a writer, photographer and web editor. Her short stories have featured in a number of publications and as well as currently working on some new stories, she is also researching her first novel. By day Jane works on a large website, writing and designing content, and researching user needs. She lives in Manchester with her partner Raymond, six cats and a slightly bemused dog. She spends far too much time on Twitter, where you can follow her: @janewright

Mother's Milk Books
is an independent press, founded and managed by
at-home mother, Dr Teika Bellamy.

The aim of the press is to celebrate femininity
and empathy through images and words,
with a view to normalizing breastfeeding.
The annual Mother's Milk Books Writing Prize, which
welcomes poetry and prose from both adults and children,
runs from September to mid-January.
Mother's Milk Books also produces and sells art
and poetry prints, as well as greetings cards.
For more information about the press, and to make purchases
from the online store,
please visit: www.mothersmilkbooks.com